WEIRDOS
OF THE UNIVERSE,
UNITE!

WEIRDOS
OF THE UNIVERSE,
UNITE!

PAMELA F. SERVICE

A Jean Karl Book

ATHENEUM **1992** **NEW YORK**
Macmillan Canada
TORONTO
Maxwell Macmillan International
NEW YORK OXFORD SINGAPORE SYDNEY

Atheneum
Macmillan Publishing Company
866 Third Avenue
New York, NY 10022

Maxwell Macmillan Canada, Inc.
1200 Eglinton Avenue East
Suite 200
Don Mills, Ontario M3C 3N1

Macmillan Publishing Company is part of the Maxwell Communication Group of Companies.

First edition

Printed in the United States of America

10   9   8   7   6   5   4   3   2   1

The text of this book is set in 12/14 Times Roman

LIBRARY OF CONGRESS CATALOGING-IN-PUBLICATION DATA

Service, Pamela F.
    Weirdos of the universe, unite! / Pamela Service.
        p.   cm.
    ''A Jean Karl book.''
    Summary: Dedicated weirdos Mandy and Owen accidentally summon up five mythological beings, who need their aid in defending Earth from space invaders.
    ISBN 0–689–31746–8
    [1. Fantasy.]   I. Title.
    PZ7.S4885We   1992
    [Fic]—dc20   91–18438

For Jenny and Kathy

CONTENTS

CHAPTER 1

WEIRD

"Kid, are you ever weird!"

Mandy turned around and squinted across the playground. She wanted to see just who Tracy's crowd was calling weird now.

It looked like Owen what's-his-name, the new boy. The short black kid who'd moved here last month from California or someplace. She'd never paid him much attention, but if Tracy Trueblood and her followers were bothering to call him weird, he must have some promise.

Owen didn't seem too put down by this reception, but then he always looked pretty laid back. Laughing, he stood amid the group of kids and held something round and tannish in his hands.

"Really, Owen," Amy said, echoing her friend Tracy, "you're just too weird."

"Yeah," Kevin added. "Beam on back to California and eat sprouts. Feed some to your furry friend too."

They all laughed at this, but Owen only shrugged and put whatever he was holding back in his jacket pocket.

1

"Sorry you guys don't have better taste," he said casually. "But, hey, that's your problem, not mine."

He began strolling away from the Trueblood corner of the playground, moving roughly in Mandy's direction. She smiled. What a golden opportunity. All she had to do was step up and talk to him while some of Tracy's group was still watching, and she'd win another point in this year's campaign.

Last year, she blushed to recall, her aim had been to be accepted into Tracy Trueblood's circle. She'd worn all the right clothes, done her hair in just the right way, and even sprinkled her talk with their snide little phrases. It had worked for a couple of months, but then somehow they'd seen through her. Maybe it had to do with her not being catty enough about one of the class's dumpier girls. Anyway, she'd been drummed out of the clique, a memory Mandy now delighted in. She'd really been freed, freed to be herself.

All summer Mandy had planned her new self. She'd be utterly unique, utterly weird. If something was in fashion with Tracy's group or any other, she wouldn't wear it, do it, or say it. Weirdness wasn't easy, she'd discovered once school started again. She had to work at it, always alert to keep herself from doing anything stylish or ordinary. And here, she thought while watching Owen cross the playground, might be a fellow crusader.

Pushing her glasses back along her nose, she shoved herself off from the chain-link fence where she'd been leaning. Conspicuously flapping her colorful Peruvian poncho, she walked right up to him.

"Hey, Owen, you sure freaked out those airheads. How'd you do it?"

Owen smiled up at her. "Oh, I just showed them Tribble. But obviously he was wasted on them."

2

He reached into his pocket and brought out a large ball of tan fur. It started making soft trilling noises. Mandy stared at it, fascinated.

" 'Star Trek,' right?'' Mandy grinned. They reran that episode on TV so often you couldn't miss it, fan or not.

"Right."

"How do you make it purr like that?"

"It likes me." Owen laughed. "Nah, it's got batteries."

"That's first-class weird," Mandy said admiringly. She thought a moment, then jumped to a decision. "Owen, how would you like to join a secret club I've founded? It's called WEIRD. Looks like you qualify."

A thoughtful look settled on his face. "Maybe. I'd have to hear more about it. I'm not much of a joiner."

Mandy nodded. Good material, all right. "Well, it's . . ." The bell bleated over the playground. "Rats. Tell you about it later." Together they walked back to the school building, Mandy casting a superior sneer toward Tracy's corner.

Throughout the rest of the day, Mandy worried about whether expanding her club of one was really a good idea. But then, what good was leading a crusade if you didn't have any followers?

When the day's final bell rang, she still wasn't certain, but then, ahead of her in the hall, she saw Owen walking toward the main doorway where Tracy and friends were gathering. The opportunity was too good to pass up.

She hurried to catch up, then laid a friendly hand on Owen's shoulder. Loudly enough for the others to hear, she said, "Let's walk home together, Owen, so I can tell you more about the secret club. It's got a lot of important rules and stuff." She heard some giggling comments behind her and, smiling inside, acted as if she hadn't.

When they got outside, Owen threw her a lazy grin. "Is that one of them?"

"Huh?"

"One of the important rules. Doing things that bug Tracy and crew."

"Yeah." Mandy smiled back. This kid was sharp. "That's one of them: Never miss a chance to make an impression. But there're lots of others. Like: Don't do anything in an ordinary way when there's a weirder way possible. Also: Make a point of saying you dislike whatever most people like, and the other way around."

As they crossed the playground to the schoolyard gate, Owen nodded seriously. "You seem to have made quite a study of it."

"I have. It's become my cause! Defend the right to be weird! It's a real uphill battle too."

The street with its gold-tinged maples led them into the town square. The little town of Hermes, Iowa, wasn't even a county seat, so there was no important-looking courthouse in the center of their square. What it did have was a tall column on which a running figure of the Greek god Hermes, the town's namesake, was eternally balanced on one foot. Summer and winter, the greenish bronze statue wore only a helmet, sandals with wings sprouting out the back, and a cloth tied around his waist.

At the base of the column, they stopped to readjust their backpacks. "You live in Olympia Towers too, don't you?" Mandy asked.

"Yeah, on the fifth floor."

"Oh. I live on the seventh." She was very proud of living on the top floor of the tallest apartment building in town. Continuing along the familiar route, she asked, "So what do you say? Do you want to be a member of WEIRD?"

4

Owen shrugged. "Sure, I guess so. How many members does that make now? Two?"

She nodded. "We have to be selective. Most people aren't anywhere near weird enough."

"So, have we got a secret handshake or something?"

Mandy nodded eagerly, glad she'd worked that out over the summer. "There's a secret sign for recognizing fellow members. It's holding up three fingers like this. Looks innocent enough, but it's really the sign of the *W*."

As Owen tried it, she continued. "Then for the handshake, each person makes the *W* sign and then joins them together like this." She demonstrated with her own hands, then tried it with Owen until they got it right.

"Okay, that's cool," Owen said at last, "but what does WEIRD stand for?"

Mandy looked blank. "Just *weird*, I guess."

"But the letters have got to stand for something different, like NASA—National Aeronautics and Space Administration. Or MADD—Mothers Against Drunk Driving."

"Oh, well, I haven't really thought about the letters standing for anything."

"Got to if it's a real organization," Owen said, looking up at the seven stories of Olympia Towers, now rising ahead of them. "Let's stop at my place, grab a snack, and work this thing out."

Mandy agreed since she had to walk past his floor anyway—elevators being too nonweird. Besides, if he was going to join her club, she'd best get to know him better. Seeing someone's home was a good way to do that.

As soon as she stepped into Owen's apartment, however, she felt a lot more confused than informed. It had to have the same layout as her own apartment above, but it looked about as strange as someplace shown in *National Geo-*

graphic. Even as they'd walked down the hall, there'd been an odd smell, and when they'd opened the apartment door a cloud of exotic odor had engulfed them.

In astonishment, Mandy looked at the living room. No couch, no coffee table, no television. In fact, no furniture at all. The floor was covered with dark-colored rugs in squiggly patterns, and on the walls were posters and cloth hangings showing nasty-looking creatures. Most were fat with snarly snouts and assorted horns and tusks. A couple were probably supposed to be fairly good-looking women, but even they had more than the usual number of arms.

But the oddest thing in the room was its single occupant. Sitting cross-legged on a rug was a slender black woman wearing a baggy orange pantsuit. Under a soft, full cloud of black hair, her eyes were closed and she seemed to be listening intently to music coming from some speakers in the corner of the room. At least Mandy guessed it was music. There were drums and jingly things and an occasional bleat like a cow in pain. And there were voices too, deep voices that sort of overlapped each other until it made the inside of her skull itch. It made her think of when she had woken up after her tonsil operation and all the nurses had sounded hollow and echoey and made no sense at all.

Owen seemed to take the whole scene in stride and tiptoed through the room to the kitchen. Mandy followed, and when he'd closed the door, she looked curiously around. It was a pretty normal kitchen. At least it had furniture and there was a TV on the counter.

Rummaging in the refrigerator, Owen asked, "What do you want to eat?"

"Uh," Mandy said, struggling to bring back her thoughts, "whatever you've got. Was that your mother?"

"Yeah. She was meditating, or I'd have introduced you."

"Medicating? She's on some sort of medicine?"

"*Meditating*, not medicating. She's trying to clear her mind and fill it with eternal truths or something. How about some carob pudding and graham crackers? The rest of this stuff looks too healthful."

"Fine. What kind of eternal truths?"

Owen plunked down a quivering bowl of chocolate-colored pudding on the table, then added a box of organic oat bran graham crackers. "Don't know. Mom says I'll have to meditate to find out, but all I'd really like to learn is the levitating part. She can't do it yet, but I keep watching."

"What's that?"

"Levitating's when you kind of rise up off the floor and float around the room. I think that'd be cool. I'd like to see what would happen if I started doing that in a spelling quiz or something."

Mandy giggled. "Tracy Trueblood would just pass out. How long will your mom have to do this meditating before she can do the floating?"

Owen shrugged and started scooping the pudding into bowls. "Don't know, but I bet she'll be into something else before she gets that far."

"What do you mean?" Cautiously Mandy tasted the pudding, then took a second mouthful. Whatever this carob stuff was, it tasted almost like chocolate. Almost but not quite.

"Oh, she goes through phases. When I was little, it was African. She was into getting back to our roots. That wasn't bad. We had African music on all the time, and I got to wear wild shirts."

He plunged his hand into the box and pulled out a fistful of graham crackers. "Then she decided that just because we are black we shouldn't 'cut ourselves off from the common human experience.' So we went Japanese. That's when we got rid of all the furniture and had mats on the floor. The food was pretty yucky, but I got to take karate lessons.'' He let out a yell, karate kicked an invisible opponent, and went back for some more graham crackers. "But she decided the Japanese thing was too violent, so just before she joined the new law firm and we moved here, she went Tibetan.''

Mandy scraped up the last of her pudding, wondering if it was real Tibetan stuff or if they just had to make do. She doubted Hermes, Iowa, had a Tibetan grocery store.

"So, anyway," Owen said through a mouthful of graham crackers, "we've got to figure out what WEIRD stands for."

"Right. Down to business. Can the *W* at least stand for *weird*?''

"Sure. Weird something. Something that starts with an *E. Eternal, elephants, eager?* No, I've got it. *Entities.* Weird Entities something something something.''

"Okay, so next's an *I. "Institute, interesting.* How about just *in*? Weird Entities In . . .''

"Good!" Owen rummaged in a drawer and brought out an envelope and a stub of pencil. "Okay, Weird Entities In . . . what? Something with an *R. Real? Rightful?* Yeah. Weird Entities In *Rightful* . . .''

"*Domination!* Weird Entities In Rightful Domination. WEIRD power!''

"Right on!" Owen grinned, holding up the *W* sign. They shook the secret handshake across empty pudding bowls.

A little later, when Mandy opened the door to her own apartment, she was overwhelmed by ordinariness. Ordinary furniture, ordinary pictures on the wall, an ordinary mother fixing what would no doubt be an ordinary dinner, even an

8

ordinary baby brother playing on the rug. Not even any incense. Boy, did she have a lot to overcome.

She shook her head and flopped down her schoolbag. Owen, she realized, came by his weirdness naturally. Some people sure had all the luck.

CHAPTER TWO

THE ASSIGNMENT

At the end of that week Miss Emerson gave the English class an assignment. They had been studying Greek and Roman myths, and now she handed out a long list of mythical characters from various cultures. Everyone was to pick out one or two to write a paper on.

When Mandy got the list, she looked at it and frowned. She hadn't heard of most of these characters. Still, some sounded weird enough to have possibilities.

She and Owen were now regularly walking home from school together. Sometimes they held club meetings along the way or at one of their apartments to work out new rules for WEIRD. That day Mandy brought up the question of the mythology papers as soon as they left the schoolyard, suggesting they work on them together.

"I'm not sure how a member of WEIRD should handle this. Nearly all the characters on this list sound weird, so it's going to be hard to write weirder papers than the other kids."

"True." Owen tramped along thoughtfully for a moment. "But I know one thing we can do that the others won't."

"What?"

"We can start ours a lot earlier. The papers aren't due for weeks. Everyone's sure to put them off till the last moment. Then there'll be a big jam-up at the library, and no one'll be able to get the books they want. So if *we* go to the library and start working right away, our papers can be better and longer than the others, and we can even turn them in early."

"Yeah." Mandy nodded. "That'd certainly be weird for me anyway. And we'd have time to do bunches of illustrations too. I bet lots of these characters are pretty weird-looking."

"Sure to be. Let's check the library now and see how much stuff there is on these guys. That'll make it easier to choose."

They veered down another street, and soon their pace turned from a walk to a jog as the sky, which had been darkening all afternoon, began loosing a light patter of rain. When they reached the library, they sat on a bench in the front lobby and looked over Miss Emerson's now slightly damp list.

"She's got them divided into five types of mythological characters," Owen pointed out. "It'll take forever to look them all up. Let's just pick one from each group, check how much info the library's got on them, and make our choices from there. Once we do the research, we can decide who's doing a paper on what."

"Okay," Mandy said scanning the sheet. "What do you like in this first group, 'Tricksters'? Lokki—that's Norse—has a weird enough name. Or what about Spider? He's African; maybe you'd like him."

11

"Nah, for me that's not weird enough. You got to think this thing through. I'm black, so Miss Emerson will expect me to choose something African. Coyote might do, though. He's Native American, and I think I've seen books on him before."

"Right, Coyote it is. Now, what about group two: 'Heroes'? We can scrap Hercules and Achilles, they're too ordinary. How about this one, Gilgamesh? His name's plenty weird. Doesn't sound too macho though. Or what about Beowulf? I like the 'wulf' part."

Owen studied the list. "No, let's go with Siegfried. I saw an opera about him once. He was pretty dumb, but he had a cool magic sword and cape of invisibility, and he sliced up this fire-breathing dragon."

"I don't know," Mandy said, pushing back her glasses. "I kind of like dragons. But, hey, you can have him if I can have this Chinese Dragon Princess on the "Nature Spirits" list."

"Fine by me. This next group looks a lot more interesting: 'Witches, Monsters, and Evil Spirits.' Now, these dudes have got some great names: 'Grendel, British; the Three-Headed Mangus, Mongolian; Baba Yaga, Russian.' "

"Hey, I like that last one. Got a good beat to it." Mandy began snapping her fingers and twitching around on the bench. "Baba Yaga, Baba Yaga."

"Right," Owen said. "Good vibes. Now, that just leaves 'Miscellaneous.' Let's try for something really awesome. How about Apedemek the Lion God?"

"No, sounds like a disease. And Avalokiteshvara would take up half a page just writing the name. What about this one, the Horned King, Celtic? Has kind of a spooky ring to it."

"Sold!" Owen stood up glancing at his watch. "Let's run these five through the computer and see what the library has on them."

The two tromped upstairs and headed for the computer terminal at the end of the row, where they could talk without being riddled by scowling stares.

Though they were beside a window, the light was so bad that the green writing on the computer screen glowed more brightly than usual. Outside, the sky seemed as heavy and dark as lead, and a wind was lashing the trees about like orange and yellow pom-poms. On top of his column in the center of the town square, the nearly naked figure of Hermes looked as if he were racing into the wind. Mandy shivered on his behalf.

Then she looked back at the screen. Owen had already pressed SUBJECT, had entered COYOTE, and was copying down the call numbers displayed. There were quite a lot.

"Looks like one of us could do a big paper on him," Owen said, then punched in the next subject.

Mandy wasn't at all sure that being weird necessarily meant doing a lot of work. The call numbers for the Dragon Princess looked better, just three of them. Siegfried, however, had a bunch of references, and she decided she'd leave him to Owen. But she thought she could handle the seven numbers that popped up for Baba Yaga, so she carefully wrote them down. There was just one reference for the Horned King, or Wild Huntsman. Not much for a paper, but he sounded sort of interesting, so maybe she'd look him up anyway.

The thunder, which had been rumbling toward them, suddenly cracked near at hand. Both children jumped, then stared out the window as the sky seemed to split open and let loose a solid curtain of rain.

13

"The sensible thing," Owen said, "would be to stay here until it lets up."

Mandy grinned. "Which means the weird thing would be to walk home now. We can check out these books tomorrow."

Owen grinned back and pushed the OUT button on the computer.

Just then the world exploded with sound. A white spear of lightning jabbed down at the Hermes pillar, then bounced across to the library, nearly blinding them. When the light and sound faded, everything was much darker than before. All the lights in the library were out. Almost all. The computer screen in front of them glowed more intensely than ever.

In vibrant green letters it asked, "Is your selection complete?" Automatically Owen punched the NO button, though he hadn't seen these computers ask that before. Instead of fading, the screen flickered, then glowed with a new message.

"Do you wish further information on these subjects for a final selection?" Mandy and Owen looked at each other and shrugged. This machine was a lot fancier than they remembered. Mandy pushed the YES button.

The screen flickered again, then began flashing "Meet sunset, Hermes."

Owen stared at the screen. "That's gibberish. The lightning must have scrambled it."

Just then the lights in the rest of the library came back on and their own screen faded to black. Mandy looked out the window. "Heck, the rain's stopped. Well, at least we can walk in all the puddles."

When they stepped out of the library's front door, those puddles were reflecting the purple and scarlet of a fiery sunset. On the street, cars splashed through the water, sending up rooster-tails of spray.

Happily Mandy and Owen tried to do the same as they ran across the street to the little concrete island in the center of the town square. They walked to the other side and were ready to jump into the street again when a young man stepped out from behind the base of the pillar.

The first thing Mandy noticed about him was that he wasn't wearing a thing—except for some sort of metal hat on his head and a white towel tied precariously about his waist. He didn't even have shoes on, but from the back of his heels small feathery wings seemed to grow. They were flapping gently.

CHAPTER THREE

WINGED FEET AND A DOG

With a surprised smile, the near-naked fellow with the winged feet stared at the two children. "Well. In disguise, I see. Good idea, ladies, but where is the other one?"

"What other one?" Mandy responded before she remembered she wasn't supposed to talk to strangers. And he certainly was strange.

"I mean, there are always three of you. I thought you usually stayed together."

"No, sir," Owen said, edging away. "There's just us two, and Tribble, of course." He giggled nervously, looking around for the best direction to run.

"Tribble? Who's that, then?"

Humor him, Owen thought as he pulled the tan fur ball out of his pocket and flipped on the purring switch. "See, just a tribble, perfectly harmless. But we're in a hurry. Got to go."

The young man laughed, not particularly maniacally. "You constantly astound me, ladies, an even cleverer disguise. No one would ever recognize the three of you. Yes,

I will be brief. I understand you need more information before you make your final selection?''

Who does this guy think we are? Mandy wondered. He looks at a boy, a girl, and a toy tribble, and sees three ladies. A real nut case!

She smiled weakly. ''Oh, yes, one can always use more information. But not now, we're in a big hurry, you see.'' She stepped casually toward the curb.

''Yes, that's fine, ladies. I will set up individual interviews if you like. There is no extreme hurry, of course. The enemy needs to be much nearer to our sphere of power before we can take any action.''

Owen stuffed the tribble back into his pocket and grabbed Mandy's hand. ''Great. Yes, that sure is good news. No hurry. Now, you just set up those interviews, and we'll be on our way.'' With a hearty wave he turned and walked swiftly across the street, Mandy right beside him. When they reached the other side, they looked at each other and both whispered, ''Run!''

After a block they slowed down and looked back. No crazed towel-clad man was pounding over the sidewalk behind them. ''What do you think he was?'' Mandy asked. ''A child molester?''

''Maybe, but he didn't do any molesting. Could be just a harmless nut. Or maybe it was a practical joke. I think he was expecting someone else.''

''Yeah, three ladies.''

''Well, he sure needs his eyesight checked.'' Owen giggled. ''Let's go home.''

With occasional nervous glances over their shoulders, they hurried to their apartment building. When they neared the main door Mandy said, ''Do you think we should tell anyone about that character? You know, report him?''

Owen thought a moment, then shook his head. "No, he didn't do anything to us. There's no law against being a nut."

Vigorously Mandy nodded. "You're right. How can we claim to champion the cause of weirdness if we freak out every time we see someone else being weird?"

She raised her hand in a defiant *W* sign, and Owen solemnly did the same.

Nevertheless, Mandy found her very ordinary apartment quite comforting that evening. After helping her mother set the table, she happily played peekaboo with her baby brother and his pink bunny while her dad took his usual nap in front of the TV evening news.

Even the news was comfortingly ordinary. A big fire somewhere, but nobody got hurt. Scientists excited about discovering a new comet. The president of someplace or other visiting someplace else. Then after a dinner that was about the height of ordinariness—chops, rice, and squash—Mandy did her homework and went to bed. Weirdness, she reminded herself, was unquestionably good, but at times it was possible to get too much of a good thing.

The next morning, when she and Owen set out for school, they avoided mentioning the strange encounter. But when they saw the Hermes column, Owen asked quietly, "Do you remember that last message on the library computer?"

"You mean that gibberish after the storm?"

"Yeah, after it asked if we had made our selection and wanted.any more information. It said, 'Meet sunset, Hermes.' Last night, I got to thinking. Suppose it wasn't gibberish? Suppose it was meant to say something like 'Meet me at sunset by the Hermes column'?"

Mandy stared at him. "Come on. You think that guy in

the towel is a mad computer hacker sending messages through the library computers?''

''Well, all the other lights and computers went off after the lightning struck. Maybe he was sending a message somewhere else, and because of the lightning it got transferred to our terminal.''

''That is pretty weird.''

Owen grinned. ''Thank you. I do my best. But it's also kind of dumb. Let's talk about something else.''

Mandy heartily agreed and cast around for a subject. For the first time she really looked at a dog she'd been vaguely aware of for some time. ''Have you noticed that dog? It seems to be following us.''

It was smaller than a German shepherd but had the same erect ears and thick neat fur, only the coat was a sort of golden gray. Its bushy tail waved jauntily back and forth as it watched them, an open-mouthed, cocky grin on its face.

''Looks friendly enough,'' Owen said. ''Maybe he just smells your breakfast.''

''Or yours.''

''Nah. You probably had something like bacon and eggs. I had Tibetan millet porridge and goat's milk. Yucko. Still, it's better than the Japanese period with the seaweed and raw fish. Let's get a move on or we'll be late.''

They continued on their way, the dog trotting merrily behind them. Mandy kept looking back at it and frowning. ''I wish it would stop following us. Wherever its home is, we're probably leading it farther and farther away from it.''

Finally they stopped, turned around, and began yelling, ''Shoo! Go away! Go home, dog!'' Owen jumped up and down, waving his arms like a windmill, and Mandy flapped the velvet evening cape she'd chosen to wear that day. The dog just sat watching them, and when they started walking again, it got up and followed. After several more attempts, they gave up and ran for school. They were almost late.

Rushing across the schoolyard, they entered the main door as the last bell was ringing. Then, galloping down the hall, they made it to Miss Emerson's room just as she was beginning to call roll.

Owen hadn't even reached his seat, however, when the teacher stopped and looked at him sternly. "Owen, need I remind you that we do not bring pets to school?" Owen swiveled around and saw the grayish dog standing right behind him.

"Yikes! I mean, he's not my dog. He just followed us." He looked pleadingly across the room to where Mandy was sitting.

"That's right," she spoke up. "Owen doesn't have a dog."

Miss Emerson frowned as the dog sat down and looked up adoringly at Owen. "That dog seems to disagree. Please take him outside, Owen."

Exasperated, Owen tramped back out of the room, the dog following devotedly behind. Heading to the nearest outside door, he opened it, pointed, and shouted, "Out!" Obediently the dog trotted out. Yanking the door closed, Owen headed back to the classroom.

Two minutes later, Miss Emerson walked right up to his desk and said, "Owen, this is not very funny. You didn't put your dog out at all."

He looked up in horror. The dog, having walked in the front door of the classroom, was sitting in the aisle beside him. "Honest, I did, Miss Emerson. He must've come in when someone else opened a door. But, really, he isn't my dog."

"The evidence is somewhat to the contrary, Owen. But I'll give you one more chance. Take him out."

Again Owen led the devoted dog out, but this time he ran around checking that all the doors to the outside plus the two to his classroom were fully closed before he returned to his seat. They heard a few yipping howls from the playground, but Owen'd almost forgotten the animal until someone sitting by the windows began to shriek. Everyone looked around to see a dog balanced on the ground-floor window ledge wriggling its way in through an open window and sending several potted plants crashing to the floor. The room erupted in screams and giggles. Mandy and Owen both jumped up and dived for the animal, but the teacher said coldly, "Amanda, sit down. This is clearly Owen's dog. Let him take care of it."

"It's not mine, really," Owen said feeling around the animal's neck for a license and collar but not finding any.

"Don't contradict me again, young man, or I'll send you to the principal. Take him out. Cindy and Patrick, please close all the windows."

For the third time, Owen trudged down the hall, the dog following faithfully behind. "You stupid dog," he muttered. "You're getting me in a lot of trouble with these tricks. Even if I could keep a dog, I wouldn't want one who's as much of a pain as you." When once more he'd evicted the animal, he returned to his desk, ignored the snickers of Tracy and friends, and sat glowering.

At lunchtime, the dog was waiting in the playground. Owen tried to lose himself in crowds, but the animal tracked him down. He tried to run away from it, but it playfully ran after him. He and Mandy tried to trick it out the gate, but it didn't trick. However, when the end-of-period bell rang, it finally seemed to have gone. Giddy with relief, Owen raced to his classroom.

21

He could have screamed. On one side of his desk sat the dog, tongue lolling out of a grinning mouth. On the other stood Miss Emerson, definitely not grinning.

"Owen, go call home and have someone come pick up your dog."

"Can't. I think my mom's in court today. Besides, he's not my dog."

"That's it. To the principal this minute. Stupid tricks I can take, but I will not have you repeatedly lying to me." The room sank into deathly silence as Miss Emerson angrily wrote a note and thrust it at Owen.

Five minutes later, he and the dog were seated across the desk while the principal frowned over the note. "Now, young man, wouldn't it be better to admit that this is your dog?"

"But he's not! I never saw him before he followed Mandy and me to school this morning."

"Come now, stray dogs don't form attachments to strangers that quickly. We do not like your lying to us, Owen."

"But I'm not lying, I'm not!" Owen was on the verge of tears. "They don't even let us keep hamsters in our building."

"Well, then, if he's not yours, you won't mind if we call the animal shelter people to came and take him away."

"Sure. Fine, do that. Go ahead." Falteringly Owen glanced at the dog and its look of mindless devotion. "Eh, they won't kill him, will they?"

"Ah, so you do care! He *is* yours."

"No! He's not! I just don't like to see any dog get killed, stray or not."

The principal silently stared at him a moment and then thumbed through a phone book and placed a call to the animal shelter.

"There," he said when he'd hung up, "they'll be here in ten minutes. And, eh . . . don't worry, I don't think they'll kill him. *If* he's not yours, they'll try to find his owner or someone else to adopt him. He's a pretty good-looking beast. It should be easy."

He laid a hand briefly on Owen's shoulder. "Now, until they get here, I want you to shut the dog in the empty room across the hall. Then sit on the bench outside and think about the importance of obeying school rules and not lying."

"But I'm not . . ."

"Just do it."

Meekly Owen led the dog across the hall and closed him in the room. Then he sat down on the bench and fumed. What a perfectly rotten day, and now he felt even more rotten about sending that stupid dog to the animal shelter. If he didn't, though, he'd probably get expelled from school.

When the shelter people arrived, the principal came out of his office and told Owen to get the dog. This was probably the last part of the test, Owen realized. He'd better act like he didn't give a hoot what happened to the dog. Shrugging casually, he opened the door. The dog was gone.

CHAPTER FOUR

ICE CREAM AND SPACE INVADERS

Instead of the dog in the nearly empty room, there was an Indian. Or at least there was a young man with a reddish complexion, long black hair held in a headband, and wearing beaded buckskin. When the door opened, he had stopped in the middle of a leaping dance and stared at the crowd in the doorway.

The principal was the first to recover. "And who, may I ask, sir, are you?"

The man smiled a thin, lopsided smile and said, "My name is Jake Laughing Jaws. One of the teachers asked me to come and perform an authentic Indian dance for her class. I arrived early and decided to wait in here and practice. Is that all right?"

"Sure, fine," the principal sputtered. "But what about the dog? There was a dog in here, wasn't there?"

"Dog? I saw no dog."

The principal turned on Owen, looking like a volcano about to erupt. "You have deceived us again! You never put your dog in here, did you? You let him out."

"No, really, I . . ."

"Don't lie anymore, young man. You've already lied yourself into some very severe penalties." He clamped a hand on Owen's shoulder, but just then Jake Laughing Jaws stepped up.

"Do wait a moment, please. I did not realize that this was so important. There may indeed have been a dog in here. I opened all the windows because it was so stuffy, then began the summer storm chant, a very noisy one, so a dog might have escaped. I am sorry."

The principal looked from the buckskin-clothed man to Owen and then to the impatient-looking shelter people. "I'm sorry too. I'm sorry about this whole day. Owen, get back to your classroom."

When that long school day finally ended, Owen tried to avoid the Tracy Trueblood gang and their hangout by the main door, but Mandy steered him back in that direction. "Hey, don't act like you're ashamed—flaunt it! That's the weird way. Besides, you're perfectly innocent, and your brush with the law just makes you glamorous."

Owen tried not to slink when he passed the smirking knot of kids, but he felt far from glamorous. He felt even less so when outside the schoolyard they saw the dog waiting patiently on the sidewalk. Owen very nearly broke into tears.

Mandy put a firm hand on his arm. "Just ignore him. Maybe he won't recognize you."

The dog did, however, and trotted after them like an obedient soldier.

"Now what?" Owen whispered.

"Nothing. Surely he won't wait outside our building all night." They marched on, the dog at their heels.

"Let's stop for ice cream."

"I don't have any money," Owen said.

Annoyed, Mandy replied, "Then why did you suggest we stop?"

"I didn't—you did. All I said was I didn't have any money."

"I didn't say anything! I do have money, but the ice cream was your idea."

"It was not!" Owen exploded.

"True, it was mine. I do like ice cream."

Owen and Mandy stared at each other, then slowly turned around. Had the dog said that? His mouth was opening and closing. "I like ice cream, and we do need a place to talk. I suggest stopping at the shop up ahead."

The dog reared up on its hind feet and, right before their eyes, seemed to stretch and melt until there was a man standing in front of them, a man in buckskin and beads. Jake Laughing Jaws.

"More appropriate, is it not? Come along. Hunger gnaws."

Striding past them, he led the way to the ice-cream parlor. In stunned silence, they followed. The silence lasted until they were all seated around the fancy white metal table and the waitress had left with their orders. Then Owen finally erupted.

"Okay, mister, just what is going on?"

"Cool yourself. I am Coyote, a trickster, remember? That is my job, tricking folks. But I did not want to run you into any real trouble, not with that blustery gentleman with the ant-sized brain, so I changed my tale at the end. If you are looking for tricksters, however, you had better keep that in mind. Lokki, for example, plays mean. The more trouble he can lead someone into, the wider he smiles."

"Great," Owen said bitterly. "So I should thank you for making me look only partly a fool."

Mandy had been studying the sharp-faced young man. He didn't look at all like that other nut, but still . . . "I bet you're tied up with that guy with the funny feet who wears a towel."

The man's expression switched to blank, then back to wry again. "Hermes, you mean? True, he's the one who contacted me. He's convinced that you two are the three fates." A smile crinkled at the corners of his eyes and mouth. "Might I ask after your partner?"

"Tribble," Owen said impatiently, plunking his battery-powered fur ball onto the table.

"Ah," he chuckled. "Well, I could hardly swallow that tale. Still, I am not denying that you were divinely chosen. The Great Spirit, or the Fates, or whoever, clearly picked you to make the final selection. Why? I cannot say. Maybe you were simply in the right place at the right time with the right attitude. Ah, here is the ice cream."

For a time, all their attention was taken up by scoops of ice cream with layered toppings. Owen pushed aside his confusion and luxuriated in quantities of real chocolate after months of only carob.

When Mandy had reached the point of eating from duty instead of pleasure, she put down her spoon and pushed her glasses firmly along her nose. "Mr. Coyote, you have been talking, but you haven't explained a thing—like how you did that dog-to-man trick."

"I bet it's all tied up with that computer hacker at the library," Owen offered. "Laser projections, computer simulations."

"Coyote," the other corrected, ignoring Owen. "Not dog, coyote. I take whichever form I choose." He grinned slyly. "Do you want me to change again?"

Mandy imagined the waitress's reaction to seeing a dog

with its muzzle in the ice cream. She shook her head. "No, I believe you."

Owen put down his own spoon and tried to give the man an intimidating stare. "But I don't believe you're not in cahoots with that computer hacker. Admit it, there's something big and diabolical going on, isn't there?"

Coyote leaned back and patted his stomach, still lean-looking under the buckskins. "Oh, there is certainly something big and diabolical going on. That is what all this is about. But I do not mingle with computers. They are not a part of my belief system."

Abruptly he leaned forward again, flinty black eyes gleaming in his thin, ruddy face. "Now, let us not dance around the bush. What I need from you two—or rather you three," he said, patting the tribble and setting off the batteries, "is a decision. As a trickster, how do I rate? Am I what you want or not?"

Owen leaned forward too, trying to stare into the other's eyes in a manly, challenging sort of way. "And if we tell you, you'll leave and stop badgering us?"

"Of course." The man's fierce expression dissolved into a grin. "It is far too built up around here. Do you think this is the sort of place where Coyote would deliberately loiter?"

The two children exchanged looks, and Mandy forced a humoring smile on her face. "Well, yes, Mr. Coyote, you're a very good trickster. Don't you think so, Owen?"

"Oh, yes, the best anyone could want."

The man stood up, the lopsided grin back on his face. "Then that is settled." He nodded and walked up to the counter to deal with the bill. Then, as he headed to the door, he threw them a jaunty wave and called, "See you."

Owen looked at Mandy and said darkly, "I hope he meant that in the good-bye sense."

She nodded, crumpling up her napkin and jamming it in the empty glass. "Talk about weird characters. I wonder how he *did* do that changing trick."

"Computers and laser projections. Got to be."

Looking out the window, they saw a gray, doglike animal, trotting jauntily down the sidewalk, waving its bushy tail from side to side.

As they started to leave, they discovered that what he'd been doing at the counter was telling the waitress that the two children were paying for it all. Angrily Mandy plunked out nearly every cent she had. Trickster, indeed.

For several days Mandy and Owen dreaded seeing that dog again. But when it didn't show up outside their apartment building or at school or anywhere between, they gratefully pushed the whole bizarre episode to the back of their minds and focused again on the real world.

The big excitement of the moment was the upcoming Halloween haunted house. This year it was not going to be in the school gym. Mr. Johnson, one of the teachers, had said that the kids could use the old abandoned farmhouse on his property north of town. This was going to be the best haunted house ever, and the older kids, who were always in charge of the event, were buzzing with plans.

Pretty soon, however, it became clear that Tracy Trueblood and her crew had taken over most of the planning and were running most of the committees. They let others take part if they asked very nicely.

Mandy and Owen had no intention of asking at all and decided that if everyone else was intensely interested in the haunted house, the proper WEIRD thing to do was to show no interest whatsoever. This they did rather grudgingly.

There came a day, however, when even the greatest-ever haunted house lost its position as the center of attention.

That day began ordinarily enough, but by the middle of the morning the teachers were passing nervously whispered messages back and forth. Then three separate sets of parents arrived at the school and demanded to take their children out so they could escape from the space invaders.

Rumors spread like wildfire. Space invaders had landed. They had taken over all the big cities. No, they hadn't landed, but they were threatening to do so. The new comet scientists had discovered was really an invading spaceship. A fleet of spaceships was orbiting Earth, had taken over the planet's computers, and was ordering everybody to surrender.

Teachers with strained, worried expressions kept denying everything. Nobody believed them and kept spreading more and more elaborate rumors. By lunchtime, excitement had turned to near panic. Nobody could eat a thing in the cafeteria except for the pineapple upside-down cake. The rest of the food, particularly the Jell-O salad and meatballs, made ideal ammunition for battles with imagined space invaders. Finally the principal came on the public-address system and tried to calm everyone down. There was no invasion from space. All that had happened was that some super computer hacker had somehow managed to link into computers all over the world and had sent a prank message about how a giant spaceship was on its way to Earth to take over and how the spaceship weapons were so great that resistance was useless.

Of course, the principal stressed, this was just a stupid, childish hoax. At first there had been some panic, but now all the computer systems were back to normal and the authorities were vigorously seeking the criminal. Now everyone should calm down, forget about it, and go back to class.

The halls on the way back to class were alive with

excited talk, but Owen and Mandy spoke in whispers. "You don't suppose—" Owen began.

"—it's the same computer hacker?" Mandy completed for him.

"Couldn't be, though, could it? I mean, one week he takes over one computer at the Hermes, Iowa, public library, and the next he's taking over every one in the world. That's a pretty fast learner."

"Yeah, it's probably someone entirely different," Mandy agreed. "But then, that Coyote guy did say there was something big and diabolical going on."

"That's right, he did." Owen thought a moment. "Should we tell the police, do you think?"

"And what do we tell them? Look for a werecoyote who hangs around ice-cream parlors?"

They both looked glum for a moment; then suddenly Mandy giggled. "Well, we know where to tell them to look for the guy in the towel. Wouldn't the police be impressed if we told them to check out the top of the column in the center of Hermes, Iowa."

They both laughed very loudly, showing each other what a perfectly silly idea they thought that was.

CHAPTER FIVE

SWORDS AND DRAGONS

For several days, the nightly news was filled with speculations about the mysterious computer hacker. Worldwide efforts were launched to track him down, although they concentrated on English-speaking countries since that was the language the "message" had used. Politicians called for investigations, computer experts were interviewed, and so were small cult groups that claimed that the end of the world really was at hand or that space people were indeed on board the new comet. Then astronomers were interviewed explaining that comets were balls of ice and could not carry space invaders.

After a while it all became rather boring and people's attention began shifting back to the real world.

Even Owen and Mandy forgot their worry about computer hackers and decided that if they were going to produce mythology papers good enough to be weird, they'd better get to work. So they checked a large stack of books out of the library and divided up the task. Owen was to read the ones about Coyote and Baba Yaga, while Mandy, feeling partial to royalty, took the Dragon Princess and the Horned

King. They split the stuff on Siegfried since there was so much of it. Then once they'd done the research, they'd decide who was going to write what.

It was their common ground, the Norse hero, that they were discussing one day walking home from school. "The problem is," Owen was saying, shaking his head, "there're so many different versions of his myths. Each one has something different from the others."

"Yeah, it's confusing," Mandy admitted. "But even if he's doing different stuff, he's basically the same kind of guy in all of them. A dumb jock—all brawn and no brains. Those awful things that kept happening wouldn't have if he'd had an ounce of smarts."

By this time, the two were strolling down a residential street near the Hermes business section. On one corner stood the Valhalla Funeral Home, a gloomy sort of place to which they usually paid little attention. But today Owen noticed something.

"Look, they've put a new statue by the doorway. Looks like one of those Norse guys in the books."

"Guess it's supposed to go with the name," Mandy said, proud to have learned that Valhalla was some sort of Norse heaven.

Together they examined the carved sword and armor and the realistic-looking hair and beard. Together too, they yelped and jumped back. The statue was also examining them.

A smile spread over the ruggedly handsome face, and the statue, which was clearly not a statue, shook himself like a wet dog.

"By all the gods, what a relief to abandon that pose! I am a man of action, not of sneaking disguises. And you, despite your guise of youth, I sense, are the Norns."

"The whose?" Owen and Mandy both said while edging away from the man.

"The Norns, as well you know. Only I was always of the belief that there were three of you."

Owen sighed and glanced at Mandy. It was like a TV rerun. "Don't you mean Fates? And the third one's in here," he said patting his jacket pocket with the tribble inside.

"Fates, Norns, it is all the same," the big man said heartily. "Even you wise ones with all your disguises cannot fool Siegfried. Just as no evildoer can hope to stand against my trusty sword, Notung!"

With one sweeping motion he unsheathed his jewel-encrusted sword and flourished it over his head. The two children ducked and began looking about for help. But no helpful passersby were in sight.

"Right," Mandy said from where she crouched on the sidewalk. "Why, the two of us . . . the three of us were just talking about you."

"That's so," Owen added from where he cowered beside her. "We were talking about what a terrific hero you are. It's just too bad we can't stay and talk to you about it longer."

"It's real busy being a Norn," Mandy said as, still half crouching, she and Owen edged their way to the curb. Glancing at traffic and seeing a car slowing for the stop sign, they pelted across the street.

From behind them the warrior gave a bloodcurdling yell. "Beware the monster bearing down on you! But fear not! I will slay it!"

As they jumped onto the far curb, the two children looked around. The blue Chevette was stopping, and Siegfried, muscular legs braced apart, raised his sword over his head with both hands and brought it flashing downward. It cut through the front end of the car as if it were bread. A six-inch slice of bumper, grille, and headlights clattered forward onto the crosswalk.

For a second Mandy and Owen stared in horror, then they turned and ran up the street as if their lives depended on it—which seemed a very strong possibility with this madman behind them.

Running without thinking, they soon found themselves beyond the edge of town. Mandy, who had been slightly out in front, stumbled to a halt in a weedy meadow, gasping for breath. She was afraid to turn around until she heard Owen give a sharp moan.

The big blond warrior in bronze-studded armor was loping easily along their trail, his broad-bladed sword flashing in one hand.

"Ho there, Norns," he cried cheerily. "Have no fear. I decapitated the beast, scaly fire-breathing monster that it was. Its keeper was indeed wroth, but a mere brandishing of trusty Notung here, and the cowardly wretch fled away. And now, I see you are testing my fleetness of foot. A wise plan if you seek the greatest of heroes, which indeed I am. Have you heard tell how I dispatched the treacherous Danes or perhaps heard a recounting of my battle with the fearsome dragon, Fafner?"

"Oh, yes, great feats," Owen said. He had read enough to know they did not want this blowhard recounting battles.

"But no doubt you are now thinking, 'Is this Siegfried as great as other heroes?' Well, I assure you, there is not, in all the universe, another Otherworld that boasts so great a hero as I. Gilgamesh is a worrywart, Odysseus is a sly sneak, and Arthur has too many family troubles. But I, Siegfried the Mighty, with my trusty Notung at my side, am just what you need!"

"Yes, yes, I'm sure you are," Mandy said. "But we also need to be going home just now."

"Ah," the man boomed, slapping his chest, "then I, Siegfried, am the hero you choose?"

Mandy and Owen looked at each other, suddenly guessing what this big bruiser was after. "Oh, yes, indeed you are," Owen said. "Without a doubt you are our choice."

"Well, now that that's settled," Mandy added brightly, "maybe we should all be on our way."

Resolutely, Siegfried slammed his sword back into its richly decorated scabbard. "Yes, truly, it is time that . . . Now, what is that yonder, do you think?"

They followed his gaze upward. High in the west, a portion of the sky seemed to be boiling. Clouds churned and swirled in a writhing knot. And it was coming closer. A whole lot closer to the ground than clouds ought to come, Mandy thought. She was just turning to Owen to whisper that this would be a good time to slip away when she saw his eyes suddenly widen.

"Look!"

She did. Part of the vapor had thinned, and in the midst of the seething cloud was something. Something large and black. It had eyes. It had a long, shiny body. It looked, in fact, very much like a dragon.

The two of them might as well have been rooted for all that they were able to run. They stood staring as the boiling cloud dropped lower and lower until it actually settled onto the far end of their meadow. Then the whole thing began thinning out like mist, and from its midst stepped what was unquestionably a large black dragon.

Beside them Siegfried uttered a barbaric growl and drew out his sword again. "At last, an opponent truly worthy of my valor! Observe, great Norns, how nobly I defend you. I excel at dispatching dragons."

Mandy admitted that this looked a lot more like something one needed to be defended from than a blue Chevette. But they'd really be a lot smarter to clear out altogether. The trouble was, this exotic, glimmering dragon was absolutely fascinating. They stood watching its approach as if mesmerized.

It was as long as maybe five horses standing end to end, not counting the tail, which snaked along behind for about the same length. Its legs were not long but were graceful, almost like those of a muscular bird, and they ended in wicked-looking claws. But it was the head that was the most compelling. Riding on the end of a long, weaving neck, it was shaped more like a horse's head than a snake's, and the golden eyes were very large and intelligent. Its nostrils glowed a quiet red as did its slightly open mouth, which showed an array of inward-curving teeth like a viper's. Between these a forked black tongue flicked.

The creature was covered in gleaming black scales, except for hairy tufts on its ears and luxuriant silver whiskers, which drooped catlike from its muzzle. Swinging from both ears were what looked like huge black pearls about the size of basketballs.

When it had come within twenty feet of them, the creature smiled, showing even more saberlike teeth, and said in a low, melodic voice, "I couldn't believe it, Siegfried, when I heard that you were also among the chosen. But it seems that my worst fears are confirmed. I really do doubt that this endeavor is big enough for both of us."

Siegfried stood, deftly tossing his gleaming sword from hand to hand. "Fret not, dragon, you need not fear sharing it with me. For I, Siegfried, Dragon Slayer, will dispatch you right here and now."

"Dragon Slayer?" the scaly beast hissed. "Hardly an honorable title, Deceitful One. You could not even slay Fafner in a fair fight! No, you waited until the poor dragon ambled down to his drinking pool, then stuck your sword up from the crevasse where you lurked and slit his belly as he walked over. A poor shadow of a hero you are!" The dragon spat in disgust, a steaming glob that charred the grass where it hit.

"That is only one version of the story," Siegfried protested, "and a viciously distorted one. Though that gold-hoarding miser would have deserved little better at my hands."

The dragon snorted, sending a puff of black smoke floating off on the breeze. "Well, I have not come this distance to debate mythological niceties." Suddenly the beast's head snaked around, and its large, luminous eyes stared at Owen and Mandy. "Are these the beings who made the selections?"

"Indeed, they are," Siegfried reported proudly. "They are the three Norns."

"Fool! You cannot even count, let alone recognize mortal children when they stand before you."

Wordlessly, Owen brought out his purring tribble and held it up. Somehow it felt safer being mistaken for Norns, whatever they were, than for two eatable children.

"Ah, so," the dragon said, nodding. "Three, then. And if you are indeed the honorable beings charged with choosing, it is not for me to question the order of things. We must all follow our duty."

"And my duty, worm," Siegfried shouted, "is to slay you!"

Sitting back, the dragon breathed steamily on one set of front claws until they gleamed like knife blades. "Perhaps. Or perhaps my destiny is to slay you."

Owen turned to Mandy and whispered, "This is getting out of hand."

She nodded. "That car with its front end off will give the police fits enough. They don't need to also find a hacked dragon body or a shredded Norse hero."

Owen cleared his throat and stepped forward, immediately regretting it as the dragon's great golden eyes turned his way. In a very squeaky voice he said, "Hey, we don't think it's anybody's duty to be slaying anybody else right now."

Black lids slid down over the eyes for a thoughtful moment, then popped up again. "Mortal or not, it is obvious that these youngsters have been selected for their wisdom." The dragon took a few rattling steps forward and lowered its head closer to Owen, who shrank back until he bumped into Mandy. "You are, of course, correct, honorable youth. Personal quarrels can be settled at a more propitious moment. At present we face a common and far greater enemy."

"Absolutely," Mandy said, having no idea what the creature meant but deciding it was better to be agreeable.

"And," the dragon continued, "since I am now conversing with mortals, politeness demands my assuming a less intimidating shape."

A mist began seeping from the body of the dragon. It thickened and darkened like smoke until nothing could be seen through it. Then gradually the cloud shrank and wafted away, leaving only one small human-looking woman.

She was very petite and basically Asian looking. Long, straight black hair and soft dark eyes. But she still held a touch of fierceness about her. Clothed in scaly black armor, she had a curved sword hanging at her side and a quiver of arrows slung over her shoulder. In one hand she clutched a bow. The helmet on her head had two tufted spikes like the dragon's ears.

Black pearl earrings swayed as she bowed her head. "Greetings, Honorable Ones. My unworthy name is Lung Nu. I trust this form is less alarming."

"Oh, yes," Mandy said, though still considerably alarmed.

"As this dolt of a Norseman fails to comprehend," Lung Nu said, shooting a glare at Siegfried who was staring at her open-mouthed, "dragons of the East differ greatly from his Western sort. We are deities of great wisdom, normally peaceful unless riled"—again she glared at him—"and we have considerable control over natural forces. I, myself, in my humble way, specialize in clouds, storms, and water."

"Oh," Owen said, feeling somebody ought to say something.

"Yes, my clouds and mist you have seen, and it seems too pleasant a day to demonstrate a storm. Perhaps a nice flood?" After a brief glance around she shook her head. "Not a great deal of raw material, it seems, but we shall see."

Swiftly she drew an arrow from the quiver, strung it to the bow, and shot. In a silver arch, it shot over the weedy meadow and down into a small pond in the next field. Abruptly the water began to seeth and bubble, then rise over its banks. Within moments it was spreading over the field, sending the grazing cows into a galloping, mooing stampede. Another branch of the flood began rolling their way, sweeping over weeds, bushes, and an old rusted-out car body. Both children started to look about for high ground.

"All right, woman," Siegfried bellowed. "You need not drown the world to make a point!"

Ignoring him, the Dragon Princess looked at the other two. "Is my flood making satisfactory? Do I meet your requirements for the nature spirit you seek? If you wish, I could conjure a storm. It would require but a few moments."

"No, no, that's fine," Owen said hastily. "You're a first-class nature spirit. The best we've seen."

"Bah! If it's nature spirits you seek," Siegfried said, "my friend Thor is darned good with thunder, and *he* doesn't pose as scaly lowlife."

The princess reached for the sword hilt at her side. "I do not need my dragon shape to cut a boaster like you down to size. Come ahead. They can always find another dumb hero."

"No, no," Mandy called. "You're both fine as you are. Indispensable. Why don't you two just make a truce and be on your way?"

Lung Nu removed her hand from the hilt of her sword and turned to the children. "Once again, honorable youth, yours is the greater wisdom. For the time being, then, I pledge to refrain from doing this braggart Norseman any physical harm."

She looked smugly at Siegfried. Sullenly he shrugged and said, "All right. For the duration I won't mete out the punishment this uppity worm deserves."

"Hah! Having to endure the presence of an arrogant blockhead like you is far worse punishment than anything you could mete out with that puny toothpick of yours."

"Why, you slimy treasure hoarder! I'll have you know that . . ."

Without saying another word, the two children tiptoed to a line of trees, turned, and ran. They didn't stop until they'd reached their apartment building.

Owen leaned panting against the wall. "Mandy, I haven't any idea of what's going on. But it's a good thing they decided that business about space invaders was a hoax, because otherwise I'd say we'd already been invaded by escapees from an interstellar lunatic asylum."

Mandy had slumped down onto the front steps. "Hey, I almost wish that were the explanation."

"Yeah, that would just be weird. But this, whatever it is, is *majorly* weird."

CHAPTER SIX

THE CHICKEN HOUSE

Two days passed with no further majorly weird incidents. Mandy and Owen began feeling a little more comfortable. They still kept a sharp lookout while walking to and from school but saw nobody weirder than a man in a seedy-looking suit giving out political pamphlets on a street corner.

At school the work was fairly routine, and the real focus of interest was the upcoming haunted house. Nearly everyone in the upper grades was involved in some way, and excitement was running high. Mandy and Owen hated to admit it, but they were beginning to regret their decision not to take part. As a token of weirdness, the action seemed a little tame beside some things they'd seen of late.

After school one day while scanning the way ahead for any lurking oddities, Owen cautiously brought up the subject. "How come Mr. Johnson's letting the kids use his place for the haunted house? Doesn't he know they'll probably wreck it?"

"Oh, it's not the house he lives in, that's a cinder-block place up on the road. This other's an abandoned farmhouse somewhere else on his property."

"Hmm. So, do you know where his property is?"

Abruptly Mandy stopped and looked accusingly over the top of her glasses. "You're not thinking of abandoning ship, are you? I know it might be kind of fun to go to, but there's a principle involved. The freedom to be weird, to not follow the herd and do what everyone else is doing!"

"I know, I know. Don't go into meltdown. I wasn't thinking of actually *going* to the haunted house, not paying money for admission and all. I'd just kind of like to see what they've done with it—whether it's any good or just hokey."

"You mean, like sneaking over before Halloween and checking it out?"

Owen nodded, and they resumed walking.

Mandy's thoughtful frown slid into a smile. "Yeah, then if there were hokey bits we could give them a hard time about it without having to shell out any money."

Innocently Owen commented, "I overheard Kevin and Joel say that no one's going to be working on it this afternoon because of too many piano lessons and stuff. Besides it's almost finished already."

Without another word, Mandy changed direction, heading down a new street. Flashing the *W* sign, Owen followed.

Soon a street through a tidy new subdivision petered down to a rutted farm track. On one side, a brown harvested cornfield crackled in the breeze. A scruffy-looking pine woods huddled along the other.

"Let's cut through the trees," Mandy said. "The Johnson land starts on the other side."

Their footsteps on the carpet of fallen needles stirred up a sharp, tangy scent. The afternoon sun was warm for late October and slanted through the feathery green branches in ragged shafts of golden light.

Soon the pines began giving way to birch trees, their

slender white trunks still crowned with autumn leaves that shivered like yellow gold coins in an increasingly chilly breeze. Then the trees began to thin, and the two came to a clearing.

"Guess this is it," Mandy said. "Though it's not quite what I was remembering. Well, their fence at least is pretty cool. Got to admit that."

The fence cut them off from a view of the house, but it was worth seeing in itself. Each of the tall poles stuck in the ground was capped with a skull whose empty eye sockets glowed with hellish light.

Mandy whistled. "Pretty good effect, all right, though they shouldn't have gone off and left the lights on. Probably burn something out. Let's see what they've done inside."

As she walked to the gate, Owen, who'd been standing rooted at the edge of the clearing, ran up to her and clutched her arm. "Maybe we shouldn't. We might get caught."

"Hey, we can't miss seeing this now." She grabbed the leather handle on the gate, and it swung open with a grating squeal. "They must have worked hard for that sound. Sand in the hinges, maybe?"

She stepped into the yard, and slowly Owen followed her. The gate slammed closed behind them. Owen jumped in alarm, but Mandy didn't notice. She was staring at the house.

"Boy, I didn't realize the old Johnson place looked like this. Not your usual Iowa farmhouse. Mr. Johnson must have had ancestors who were some sort of European immigrants."

Owen had to agree, it sure looked a lot more European than midwestern. And he had an awful feeling he knew which part of Europe too. "Yeah, pretty neat, all right. Let's go now."

"Not till we've seen inside, for crying out loud."

"No, really, Mandy, I don't think we want to go inside there."

"Well, maybe *we* don't, but *I* do." She flounced off toward the front steps and had nearly stepped on the bottom one when the whole house shuddered as if it were in an earthquake, then quickly rose five feet into the air.

"How do they make it do that?" she asked in amazement, and looked at Owen. He just pointed to the space beneath the house.

She peered under it too, expecting to see huge jacks or platforms or something. Instead there were legs. Two long legs. Legs that looked as if they should belong to a giant chicken. Now they were even strutting about and scratching while the house above them turned and bobbed.

"I was afraid of this," Owen squealed. "Mandy, we've got to get out of here now. Believe me. I read the Baba Yaga stuff, and you didn't."

He'd grabbed her arm and was pulling her toward the gate when they heard a strange swishing, thumping noise from beyond the fence. Desperately Owen fumbled at the latch. The swishing grew much louder, followed by a loud thump right behind them.

"Oh, don't go. You're exactly the sort of young toothsome visitors I like best."

They spun around.

Behind them stood a narrow, high-sided wooden tub, looking as if it had been hollowed out of an upright tree trunk. Standing in it, with the tub up to her waist, was a totally hideous old woman. Beneath a frenzied mop of gray hair the well-wrinkled face was dominated by a long downturning nose and a long upturning chin. Between them, the grinning mouth showed a set of teeth so dark they might have been made out of iron. Above, two beady eyes flashed like splinters of black glass. Two gnarled hands gripped the top of a long wooden pole as if it were a canoe paddle.

"Is that . . . ," Mandy started to whisper.

"Baba Yaga," Owen whispered back, "riding in her mortar and pestle. She specializes in eating children."

"I do, indeed," the old woman said, leaning on her pole and vaulting herself to the ground. She landed with her flowery skirt and apron up over her head, revealing skinny legs and long white bloomers. After patting and fussing herself back into place, she peered forward at the two children. "My particular preference is Russian children, though I am prepared to be open-minded—and openmouthed. Hee, hee!"

She giggled to herself a moment, then sighed and shook her head. "Sad to say, however, I'm not on a gourmet sampling trip, and I rather fear you are the ones that Hermes told me to look up. But come now, there's supposed to be three. Where's the other one hiding?"

Automatically Owen brought out his battery-powered fur ball.

"Oh, a tribble!" the witch exclaimed. "How delightful. Does it eat quadrotriticale?"

Owen blinked at her. "You know about tribbles?"

"Of course I do! I'll have you know I'm one of the most ardent 'Star Trek' fans in all the Otherworlds. I know every episode backward and forward."

"You have a TV in there?" Mandy said, pointing to the brightly painted wooden cottage still bobbing about on its chicken legs.

"Well, I should think so! Not a whole lot else to do is there, between catching fat children and meddling in an occasional hero tale? Which reminds me"—she pulled a

46

long chain from a pocket and squinted at the watch that hung from one end—"it's nearly time for my favorite soap. So let's hurry this along, shall we?"

"Eh, yes," Owen said. "But what exactly is it you want us to do?"

"Aha!" Baba Yaga peered close into Owen's face. "You don't know, do you? I *thought* Hermes was off base when he said you were the three Fates. Can't fool Baba Yaga on something like that! I mean, really! The three Fates, the three Norns, Macbeth's weird sisters. They're all the same sort. Just high-class witches. And you," she said suddenly gripping Owen's shoulder with long, bony fingers, "are just two plump children and a tribble!"

Mandy jumped forward and aimed a kick at the witch's scrawny ankles. "Let go of him! The others all thought we were something more—so you'd better watch out!"

The old woman nimbly leaped aside, letting go of Owen's shoulder. "Whoa, there's no denying that one's a little spitfire, at the least."

She turned back to her odd vehicle and hoisted the long pestle up inside the mortar. "Now, don't get me wrong, dearies. Mortal or not, tasty or not, I can't deny you're something special. And I'm not dumb. I wouldn't go about eating the selection committee, would I?"

Owen rubbed his shoulder and looked at the witch. "Very kind of you, ma'am, but we really should be going now. Don't want you to miss your program."

Baba Yaga gave her mortar an affectionate pat. It hopped off toward the scrabbling chicken house and closed itself into a small shed attached to one side. "Not so fast, if you please," she said turning back to them. "You haven't given me the final word yet."

"What word?" Mandy ventured.

Baba Yaga rolled her eyes. "What a pair of half-wits! On my selection! You wanted a witch, didn't you? Will I do or not?"

"Oh, you'll do fine!" Owen blurted.

Mandy nodded her head eagerly. "Never seen a better witch. And all this—the skulls on posts, the house on chicken legs. Very well done."

The witch's face crinkled around a proud grin. "I do these things rather well, don't I? No hokey gingerbread houses for me. My German sisters are wimps."

She looked again at her watch, then picked up her skirts and scuttled toward the aimlessly gyrating house. Stamping her booted feet she chanted:

"House, house, come bend down low,
The hour's late, and it's time for my show."

Obediently the scaly chicken legs bent and the whole house settled down like a brooding hen. Baba Yaga leaped up the stairs two at a time but at the top looked back and threw them a coy smile. "Wouldn't you dear kiddies like to watch the show with me . . . and share a little snack?"

"No, thanks," Owen called.

"It's nearly dinnertime," Mandy added hastily.

"Yes, isn't it?" the witch said, licking her lips. "Well, don't be alarmed, dearies, just keeping in practice." She disappeared inside, then popped her head out again. "Don't forget to latch the gate."

Mandy and Owen were soon happy to be outside doing just that. Then they took off at a run through the birch trees and into the warmer pine woods. At the edge of the farm track, Mandy stopped and said, "Owen, I don't think there *are* birch trees growing around here."

48

"Probably not," Owen agreed as he started down the road. "But there are a lot in Russian fairy tales. It's colder there too."

Mandy groaned and followed after him. "You know something, Owen. This is getting too weird even for me. We've got to figure out what's happening."

Owen shook his head. "There's a computer hacker in it somehow. These characters we've been meeting are all ones we selected on the library computer before the lightning made everything go funny."

"Yes, but why are they all going on about whether they're the best—the ones we really want? All I wanted to do was write a stupid little mythology paper for Miss Emerson—not make a bunch of mythological weirdos feel good about themselves!"

"Maybe we're helping some kid in an alternate universe write his mythology paper. I don't know! And maybe I don't want to know. I just want it to stop."

Suddenly Mandy clutched his arm. "Owen," she whispered urgently, "we've met four of the characters we selected. But there was a fifth. The Horned King, the Wild Huntsman. There's only one book about him in the library. And I read it."

Nervously she studied the innocent-looking cornfields, then whispered even lower. "Let me tell you, we don't want to meet *him*. And if we do, don't look at him, and do not speak to him. Whatever happens, pretend he's not there."

"How come?" Owen asked, wide-eyed.

"You don't want to know."

Owen started to object. He always wanted to know everything. Then he stopped and thought about the other four on the list. Maybe there were times when being a know-it-all wasn't such a good idea.

CHAPTER SEVEN

THE FIFTH ONE

Saturday afternoon.

Mandy sat in her room brooding. This last summer she'd redecorated her room with all manner of weirdness. It hadn't been easy. What's weird to one person is someone else's "in" fad. To be universally weird, she'd decided, was a real art.

The solution, she'd decided, was putting things together that clearly did not go together no matter what your point of view. On one windowsill she'd spread a lace handkerchief an aunt had given her, and on that she'd put a rusty metal thing she'd found in someone's trash. Her walls she'd decorated with rug and wallpaper samples in clashing colors and a dead tree branch that she'd hung with pop-top lids. On her door she'd tacked up a poster of a smiling butcher, which she'd found crumpled up behind a grocery store.

Mandy's mother had not been too thrilled with the new decor, any more than she had been with Mandy's same "anything that doesn't go together" approach to her wardrobe. But she hadn't done anything as satisfying as yelling and demanding changes. She'd just shaken her head and occasionally muttered about its all being a phase Mandy was going through. As a parent, she was infuriating.

But now Mandy was ignoring her decor. Curled up on her bed, she was giving weirdness some serious thought. Not the principle of the thing. She was still committed to people's right to be as weird as they chose. The problem was, there was a whole lot more weirdness coming at her now than anyone in her right mind would choose.

Even Owen, who was laid-back about everything, was not too happy with all of this. But he couldn't figure it out anymore than she could. These "people" they'd been meeting were clearly the ones on the list they'd fed into the computer before it went wacky. But were they real? Sure, they could be seen by other people and could even dismember real cars, but were they really out of myths? And why were they all so anxious about being "selected"? Selected for what? Mandy had an uneasy feeling that it was for more than being the subject of a class paper.

She almost screamed at the sharp knock on her door. Her mother's voice said, "Owen from downstairs is here to see you, Mandy."

Like a shot, she was out of her room. Maybe he'd come up with some answers.

From his face, she could tell he'd been brooding over the same questions but was not brimming with answers. Mandy led the way out onto the apartment's little balcony where, with the doors slid closed, they could have some privacy. Below them stretched rooftops, trees, and in the distance, the taunting exclamation mark of the Hermes column.

"Mandy," Owen said seriously, when he'd plopped into the woven plastic chair, "whatever's going on is a lot bigger than we can handle. I mean, when my mom goes on health food binges, or searches for our roots, or takes up meditation, hey, I can handle that. It's just taking the real world and bending an edge of it so it makes you happier for a while. It's cool. But this . . .'' He shuddered and ran out of words.

"I know. It's like taking the real world, tearing it to pieces, and rearranging things upside down. But what are we going to do about it?''

"I've been thinking. Maybe we should take all the library books back and not do our papers at all. An *F* is just as weird as an *A*. Or maybe we should forget about being weird for once, not use the library at all, and do *C* papers on some boring Greek mythological characters we can read about in our home encyclopedias.''

Mandy nodded. "I keep worrying about how keen they are to be 'selected.' If we do choose one of them for a paper, what are they going to do? Move in with us? I can just see Baba Yaga fighting my mom over which soap operas they watch, or Siegfried laying waste to everything in town that annoys him, from slow waitresses to traffic cops. It'd be a disaster.''

"Yeah. One day of being with Coyote almost got me kicked out of school.'' Owen stood up resolutely. "All right. Lets take everything back to the library right now and not even think about those papers until the day before they're due.''

"Right!''

Within minutes Mandy's books were stuffed into a plastic shopping bag, and then the two were down in Owen's apartment collecting his. His mother was sitting on the rug again, but this time she was surrounded by a bunch of books and papers, clearly being a lawyer this afternoon and not a mystic. Mandy found it comforting to realize that "just a phase she's going through'' could be applied to adults as well as children.

"Off to the library, Mom," Owen called as he rushed back out the door. His mother nodded vaguely and hunched back over her books. Mandy wondered if being a lawyer wouldn't be easier during a phase that had furniture, desks, and bookcases at least. Maybe the next "phase" would be Early American.

The walk to the library and their brief stay there were, to their great relief, completely uneventful. Their departure was not.

After piling their books on the returns desk, they headed directly for the door. Briskly Owen walked through the metal arches that detect unchecked-out books. Abruptly they beeped at him.

Startled, he stepped back, then tried more slowly. Again the accusing beep. Looking around sheepishly at one of the staring librarians, he showed that his pockets held only one tribble and that he wasn't smuggling out any books. "Must be broken," he said to Mandy.

Just then another library patron walked through without a peep from the detector.

"Maybe it's your belt buckle or something," Mandy suggested. Then, stepping through the gate, she jumped back as it beeped at her as well. Now two librarians were glaring at them. Feeling like criminals, they slunk back into a little alcove near the doorway.

Owen unthreaded the belt from his jeans. Mandy didn't have a belt over the baggy purple sweatshirt she was wearing, but the deep pockets in her long orange skirt were jingling with pennies. She emptied these out and took off her glasses as well. "This thing must be having an identity crisis," she muttered, "and thinks it's an airport metal detector."

They were about to try again when Owen suddenly yelled, "Look!" Mandy stuck her glasses back on.

He was pointing at the screen of a computer that crouched like a smug gray animal on the alcove's one table. "Hey, you three," it flashed in vibrant green letters, "are all your selections satisfactory?"

They stared at each other. "What do we do?" Owen whispered. "I don't want any more to do with this."

"Then maybe we'd better press YES, or whoever's doing this might send us a whole new batch to choose from."

Owen groaned, then said, "Or we could not press anything and just run." He shook his head. "Nah, I bet the computer and the detector gate are in cahoots. It'd beep like crazy, and we'd be banned from the library forever."

Mandy felt panic rising in her throat, almost as if she were going to be sick. "So let's press it!" She jabbed YES.

The screen went blank, then flashed up one blazing green word: "Proceed."

Grabbing up belt and coins, they walked cautiously through the gate. Not a beep. Sighing with relief, they hurried down the library steps.

Owen glanced up at Hermes and felt like making a rude gesture at the statue smugly striding away on top of his column. But Owen decided that might get him struck down by a freak, out-of-a-clear-sky lightning bolt.

It was a beautiful day, made all the more so by their sudden feeling of liberation. The little park across the square was blazing with the oranges, reds, and yellows of fall, and the air had a crisp sparkle to it. Owen took a deep, happy breath. "Let's go back through the park."

They crossed the square and started off along the crunchy gravel paths that cut through the block-long park. Mandy looked around contentedly. A fine October Saturday, and the park was full of people. Most were down at the far end, older kids playing Frisbee while littler ones clambered over climbing frames or burrowed in the sandbox. Someone was running his dogs too. She could see three, no, four of them galloping over the grass. Big red-and-white dogs.

As they ran, the lead dog bayed and the others answered, in deep, haunting cries. On the other side of the path another pair of dogs broke from the trees and began running beside them, baying like hounds following a scent. The sound jabbed into Mandy's mind.

"Owen," she said in a strained voice, "would you describe these as red-and-white hunting hounds?"

"Yeah, I guess."

"Then, come on!" she cried, breaking into a run. "We've got to get home fast!"

She barged off the path heading for a shortcut through the trees. The dogs closed in, loping alongside them, as silent now as ghosts. Their teeth flashed white in the fading light.

Above, gray clouds had smeared their way across the formerly blue sky, and back here the trees that rose against it had already lost their leaves. In fact, there were too many trees altogether. The park wasn't that big. They should have reached the street by now.

In panic, they ran faster. Beside them, the silent hounds kept pace, their leader occasionally breaking into a hollow, buglelike cry.

Now there were other sounds too. A howling wind was rising, rattling the branches and dry dead leaves. And there was something else. Horse hooves? Yes, nearer and nearer came the sound of galloping horses. Behind them, beside them, above them.

With a shriek, Mandy lunged for Owen, dragging him to a stop, then shoving him facedown into a drift of leaves.

"Don't look up!" she screamed over the sound of wind

and horses. "Don't look at him, and don't say a thing to him!"

Owen tried to struggle up for a question, but she only pushed him back and burrowed beside him into the leaves.

Above the wind, they heard the high call of a hunting horn. It and the hoofbeats drew nearer, then stopped. There was the sound of hooves pawing at leaves and of two booted feet landing on the ground beside them. Throwing their hands over their ears could not block out the deep, commanding voice.

"So, you have selected me, have you?"

Neither cowering child said a word.

The voice throbbed in their heads like an ancient church bell. "I am the last person you could fool by playing dead, you know." The laugh that followed seemed to have risen from cold stone caverns beneath the ground.

Now the voice drew nearer and was sparked with anger. "Mortal fools, I will not be trifled with! I will not be ignored. Look at me. Look at me!"

"No!" Owen shouted, burying his head deeper into the leaves.

"Aha! An answer." Owen felt iron-hard fingers grip his shoulder. In a blur of movement, he was swept from the ground onto the back of a tall black horse. In front of him a dark, caped rider had mounted as well.

Horrified, Mandy jumped to her feet and grabbed Owen's leg to pull him down. Her heart froze with fear as she saw the rider. Then his black cloak swirled downward, a gloved hand reached out, and she was pulled up to sit between the rider and the arched black neck of his horse.

Dazed, Mandy looked around. There were other horses and riders beside them, swirling in and out of gray mists. She would have screamed, had her throat not frozen in fear.

Beneath crowns or helmets or simple headbands, all the faces were skulls. Armor and cloaks were tattered and moldering, and the mists blew in and out through the ribs of skeletal horses.

The horse beneath her, however, felt solid, as did the powerful grip on her shoulder. Again, the cold voice poured over her.

"So, mortal, you must tell me. Am I the one you seek?"

Reluctantly Mandy looked up and around. The speaker's face was dark and bearded, the upper portion hidden by a black helmet topped with a crown the color of a winter moon. From the shadowed openings two eyes smoldered like embers. Yet her gaze was drawn further upward. Rising from the helmet, like spread and clawing hands, were the massive antlers of a great stag.

"Yes," she whispered. "You are the one. You're the Horned King."

CHAPTER EIGHT

THE GATHERING

The hunting horn sounded through what had now become a vast forest. The Horned King spoke a word of command, and the huntsmen surged forward.

Desperately Owen clung to the king's waist, though he could think of no one he felt less like hugging. Deadly cold spread from the cloaked body almost numbing his arms. But he held on tightly, terrified of slipping off and being trampled under skeletal hooves.

Seated in front, Mandy's face was lashed by the horse's wind-whipped mane. Through its black veil, she glimpsed the riders surging along beside them, swords and armor clattering against stark white bones. She buried her face against the arched neck, wanting to see nothing else.

The ride seemed endless. They swept through forests and fields, occasionally glimpsing a glimmer of light in the falling dusk. It always seemed to be dusk, and mist trailed behind them like a shredded cloak. At times they did not seem to be touching the ground at all but rather passing through shifting landscapes of dark, tumbled clouds.

Mandy was half asleep when suddenly the movement beneath her changed. They were slowing, then suddenly standing still. Cautiously she opened her eyes. In the bright afternoon sun, the other riders were scarcely visible. Beyond their spectral forms, she could see the poles of an enclosing fence, each one topped with a human skull. Beyond them were the fluttering tops of birch trees, a vast sea of them.

She was about to say something when the king's black-gloved hands dropped the reins and lifted her to the ground. In moments, Owen was swept down to stand beside her. He staggered and looked around.

"I think we've been here before," he whispered.

"Someplace like. But this sure is a lot farther away than the outskirts of Hermes, Iowa."

"Ah, so you're finally here," a high voice crackled. "About time."

Mandy and Owen watched as the old woman hobbled toward them from the direction of a brightly painted wooden house. "The others have been here for ages," she said crossly, "and I'm at my wit's end. I am definitely not the hostess type."

"Call them, then," the king commanded, "so we can be under way."

"Call them yourself. That mangy desert dog's off chasing rabbits, and the empty-headed Norseman and that dragon lady are sparring behind the house—making a perfect mess of my vegetable patch. Speaking of which—will you tell your troops to get out of my flowers!"

Mandy and Owen looked where she was glaring. The half-seen skeletal huntsmen were indeed standing in a flower bed. Not that the black and bloodred blooms looked all that attractive.

Their king raised a hand and with a word dismissed his

followers. They flickered and faded completely out of sight. Then he raised his curved hunting horn to his mouth and blew a high, piercing call.

In moments a familiar grayish dog squeezed itself between two poles in the fence and came loping toward them. "Hey, take it easy with that horn, will you? Some of us have sensitive ears."

The Horned King only grunted and swung down from his horse. With a snap of his fingers, it too disappeared. Then he strode toward the house and sat down on a bench in its shade. Immediately the house stood up on chicken legs and started wandering off. The king snarled but continued sitting glumly on the bench, beginning to look somewhat transparent himself.

From beyond where the house had been, they could now see two figures stalking toward them, one tall and blond, and one small with long black hair. Both gripped swords and wore armor that was muddied and stained with green. From their faces, it was clear that the duel had gone to neither's satisfaction.

"Oh, my poor carrots and beets!" Baba Yaga wailed. "Where is that troublemaker Hermes? This was his idea. I ought to sue him, take him to people's court, have Perry Mason throw the book at him!"

Briefly the air beside them churned into a whirlwind, and suddenly Hermes was there, wearing as little as ever, Mandy noted. She wondered if maybe she and Owen could go sit down somewhere until someone decided to notice them, though actually she'd prefer it if they never did.

"Ah, good," Hermes said cheerily. "Is everyone ready to go?"

"No!" they all chorused.

Baba Yaga stamped her foot. "I'm not going anywhere until somebody gives me a better explanation of what is going on. One moment I'm minding my own business in my own Otherworld, and the next this excitable Greek is there claiming that the three Fates have selected me for an important mission. Why, any fool can see that these are two mortals and a tribble, not three Fates!''

"Well, perhaps I became a little carried away. But it was a crisis. I had just reported the threat to Zeus on Olympus, and we were trying to decide what to do, when there was an electrical storm and suddenly the Fates provided the answer. Right there in the sky before us in glowing green letters were the names of those to send on the mission. So maybe I mistook the agents for the masters. A minor error in the cosmic scheme of things.''

"You mean these persons are not the three Norns?" Siegfried said.

Lung Nu laughed derisively. "This dumb ox actually believed that a furry toy was a divinity.''

Coyote cocked his head and shot her a toothy smile. "It seems, dragon, you are not as all-wise as you think. Tribbles have been elevated to legend status in the new North American Otherworld. I know, because ours is adjacent to it. It is a little unsettling, the way new legends keep popping up there every day and shifting everyone's status around. At the moment their king is a flashy fellow named Elvis.''

Owen looked down at his tribble, thoroughly confused. Mandy decided she'd had about enough.

"Hey, just a minute, you guys.'' She flinched as all eyes turned toward her, but she carried on. "There's some major mistake going on here. Owen and I were only researching a school paper, not picking folks for some big, important mission. The computer thing was just a freak accident.''

"An accident is simply a misunderstood plan," the Dragon Princess intoned sagely.

"What old Wisdom-of-the-East here is trying to say," Coyote explained, "is that if the Great Spirit wants to work through a computer, it can."

Baba Yaga snickered. "You mortals aren't the only ones who can be up to date, you know."

Mandy hung her head. "No, we don't know, we don't know anything. This whole thing is totally confusing, and we want to go home!"

"Really, Hermes," Lung Nu said accusingly, "have you not told these children anything about the Otherworlds?"

"I am a messenger, not a teacher," he said stiffly.

"Oh, for crying out loud!" Baba Yaga said. "Someone's got to brief them." She glowered around the company and then with an elaborate sigh stared at Owen and Mandy.

"Okay, kids, it's like this. Every people on Earth, from way back up to today, have had their own set of beliefs, their own myths and legends. And each set spawns its own Otherworld. These myth worlds become real and solid but stay separate from the mortal world."

Owen's mouth had fallen open. "You mean, everyone's mythological creatures all exist somewhere?"

"In different somewheres," Lung Nu corrected. "Normally, except for gadflies like Hermes, the denizens of the Otherworlds keep themselves to themselves." She shot a cutting look across to Siegfried. "A fortunate thing too."

Mandy looked puzzled. "But nobody's believed in some of you for centuries."

Hermes shrugged. "That's their problem, not ours. Once an Otherworld is created, it is there permanently. Some, like Ancient Egypt's Otherworld, have been around for millenia. A pretty boring place, I must say, but others are still growing and changing."

"Like the one with Elvis and the tribbles," Owen ventured.

Coyote shook his head. "Can't keep pace with that one. New media characters and 'celebrities' arriving all the time. You cannot imagine a weirder group."

Mandy thought that was pretty funny coming from a talking coyote. She was about to ask a question when Siegfried said loudly, "Enough, Hermes. Your tongue runs faster than your feet. A lecture in basic mythology is fine enough, but what I want to know is why I have been called here. Obviously the Norns desire that some vile enemy be slaughtered, or they would not have summoned Siegfried the Mighty and his trusty sword, Notung. But who is it to be?"

Baba Yaga and Coyote grunted in agreement. Mandy cast a curious look toward the Horned King. He had moved into the shade of a gnarled fruit tree but was still sitting in gloomy silence.

Lung Nu cleared her throat disdainfully. "Heroes, witches, and tricksters. Shallow, decadent Westerners! All you can think about is whom shall I harass now? Obviously this is a subtle, difficult matter requiring much deep thought and effort. I, however, am not prepared to give it either until suitable refreshment is provided, perhaps some good strong tea."

"Good idea," Coyote piped up, "and some food!"

"Oh, so it's tea and snacks you want now, is it?" Baba Yaga snapped. "And I'm supposed to play hostess and serve it up, eh? Well, let me tell you, Russia's Otherworld's as good as any other."

Reaching into a pocket, she pulled out a handful of dry seeds and scattered them on the ground. Instantly they sprouted into a dozen sticklike men with long trailing mustaches. Baba Yaga spat a few words at them, and they scampered off into the house, reappearing seconds later with chairs and a table that seemed to stretch as they carried it. After another whirlwind trip, they spread the table with black bread, cheese, bowls of cucumbers and tomatoes, apples, and a big tureen of rich-smelling soup. At the center was a tall silver pot with a spigot at the bottom, which when twisted, shot out hot tea.

Baba Yaga gave them all a mocking bow, then made a quick gesture to the tree that was shading the Horned King. It pulled up its roots and shuffled over to shade one of the chairs. Shrugging, the huntsman followed.

When they were all seated and passing food and glasses of tea, Siegfried pointed suspiciously at the soup. "What's in this, old witch? Heroes do not eat plump Russian children, and that is that."

The two American children at the table stared in horror at the tureen, but Baba Yaga snarled, "It's just mushrooms and potatoes, you Norse wimp. I wouldn't waste plump children on the likes of you. But after what you and your sparring partner did to my vegetable patch, you ought to be stuck with bread and water."

As the bickering continued back and forth across the table, Mandy whispered to Owen, "I feel like I'm in a scene from *Alice in Wonderland*. Do you suppose if I yell, 'You're nothing but a pack of myths,' they'll all go away?"

"No."

"Me neither. Curiouser and curiouser." She slathered butter and jam on a hunk of bread and began listening to the conversation that was finally turning to the purpose of all this.

"The trouble is," Hermes was saying, "that although we of the Otherworlds have a real existence of our own, our ultimate survival is linked to the survival of the human world.''

''If you are trying to trick us into meddling in human politics,'' Coyote said, ''you can forget it.''

''No, no, it is not an internal threat they face. It's an external one.''

''Messenger god pauses for dramatic effect,'' Baba Yaga said dryly. ''Will you get on with it! What's the threat?''

''Space invaders,'' Hermes replied ominously. ''Their ship, disguised as an enormous comet, is on its way to Earth. They plan to wipe out anyone who resists, enslave the rest, and conquer the whole planet.''

Owen jumped up, sloshing his untouched soup onto the tablecloth. ''Boy, are you wrong! That was a hoax, some crazy computer hacker taking over all the world's computer screens.''

Hermes gave him a very schoolteacherish look. ''No, boy, *you* are wrong. That crazed master computer hacker is the *myth*, something your governments dreamed up to prevent mass panic. In time, he will probably appear in that odd Otherworld of yours. But the truth is that you mortals are about to confront a group of aliens with weapons vastly more powerful than your own. You are about to be destroyed or enslaved, and so, as a result, are we.''

Now Siegfried sprang to his feet, spilling everyone's soup, and flourished his sword. ''Never! Not if we stop them!''

Hermes gave a less than confident nod. ''That apparently is what the Fates have in mind. It does seem to be up to you. Five mythical figures, two mortal children, and a tribble.''

CHAPTER NINE

LAUNCH OF THE CHICKEN HOUSE

After that announcement, the tea party broke into a confused babble. Everyone was yelling except the Horned King, who drew himself another glass of tea and walked away from the table, the shade tree obediently trotting behind him. Hermes was jumping up and down trying to restore order, so much so that Mandy was afraid his bath-towel skirt would fall off. But then she guessed that gods who wear towels around their waists must have special magical powers to keep them there too.

Finally everyone was quiet enough for Hermes to say, "Obviously, once they arrive here, it will be too late to do much. So what you must do is intercept their ship and somehow do something to drive them away."

"Oh, that is a great plan, that is," Coyote said, flopping down on his stomach and plopping his head onto his paws. "Somehow do something."

"Well, the details I leave up to you. You can figure something out on the way."

"Wait one moment, honorable Hermes," Lung Nu said.

"Can you not tell us what these invading people are like? It is unwise to do battle with an enemy one does not know."

"Hmm, well, they are rather hard to relate to, actually. Nonhuman in shape, of course, but the big problem, from our point of view, is their imagination—or lack of it. They are a single-plane species, to say the least, a concrete, practical people who are so limited spiritually that they have no myths, no Otherworlds of their own."

"Barbarians!" Lung Nu and Siegfried said together, then looked at each other, shocked that they agreed on anything.

Coyote cocked his head at a thoughtful angle. "Hmm. This means that they probably have no clue about magic or any supernatural weapons."

Looking over his oddly mixed companions, Owen said, "Hey, I hate to tell you, but if these guys have super space lasers or something, I'm not sure magic swords and dragon clouds are going to do a bit of good."

Baba Yaga reached across the table and poked him with a bony finger. "Don't be such a Gloomy Gus. Luke Skywalker and his gang were able to destroy the Deathstar single-handed! The only one who got away was Darth Vader himself."

Owen blinked in surprise. She must have seen it on TV. He wondered if her chicken house had cable.

"Sure," Mandy pointed out, "but they did that with special effects."

"Well, that's a kind of magic, isn't it?" the witch said crossly.

Coyote sat back and began scratching his shoulder with a hind foot. "Isn't Darth Vader the tall, dark guy who wheezes a lot? I've seen him lurking around the Otherworld next door. Wouldn't be a bad man to have on this trip."

Mandy's mind reeled for a moment. Then she sputtered, "Sorry, he wasn't on our list to choose from."

"Neither was Elvis or Big Bird, or the Ninja Turtles," Owen muttered. "Miss Emerson sure missed a lot."

Hermes stood up, brushing crumbs off his towel. "Well, whatever the divine reasoning, you are the chosen ones. And it's about time you were on your way."

"And how, pray tell, are we all expected to get there?" Lung Nu asked, still sipping her tea. For the first time Mandy noticed her very long, curved fingernails. "I could, of course, fly there in my dragon form. But I trust you are not expecting me to give everyone else a ride."

"Some of us wouldn't be caught dead riding a dragon," Siegfried snarled.

Hermes cleared his throat. "Well, actually, to be honest, I was thinking Baba Yaga's house might work best."

"Oh, were you?" the witch said. "So kind of you to let me know. Listen, you meddlesome Greek, this is a one-room peasant cottage we're talking about here. I'm not exactly set up for houseguests."

Mandy gave Owen a quick look and said, "Oh, you needn't worry about us. We've got to be getting back home anyway."

"That's right," Owen said. "We wouldn't be much use to you anyhow. We haven't a shred of magic."

Hermes smiled winningly at him. "Come, young man. Don't you read your mythology? Mortals are always becoming involved in Otherworld activities."

"Right," Owen protested, "and they usually get in big trouble for it too."

"Where is your spirit, sir?" Siegfried said sternly. "Your patriotism? Your valor? Surely you thirst for the glorious chance to fight to the death for humanity!"

"That's all very well for you to say," Mandy objected. "You're immortal!"

Suddenly the Horned King was at the table again, his dark form and spread antlers looming over them. "None of us is immortal," he intoned, "if these unbelievers come." He turned his blazing eyes on Baba Yaga. "Call your house to heel, woman. We need be on our way!"

Baba Yaga's bluster shriveled, and obediently she stood up and shouted:

"House, house, come here this minute.
Bend down your door, and let us climb in it."

Instantly the house, which had been contentedly scratching away at one end of the yard, scurried over and settled itself onto the ground.

"All right, everyone in," she ordered. Then she broke into a cackling laugh. "Baba Yaga's SWAT team. I like it, sounds like a TV series. Or maybe 'Otherworld Cops.' "

The Horned King was the first inside, though he had to turn sideways to fit his antlers through the low door. Coyote leaped in after, but as Lung Nu approached the door, Baba Yaga said, "Now, just you stay in human form, young lady. I've definitely no room for dragons."

"Well said," Siegfried sneered. "No vermin allowed."

The princess hissed at him. "I will adopt any form I choose. Though I might compromise on size."

Baba Yaga shrugged and turned to Hermes. "So you're not coming, eh? Fine leader you are!"

The young man stood up straight, the wings on his feet flapping indignantly. "That is not my role, madam. I am a messenger and must be on my way."

"So, how about taking us with you?" Mandy asked.

The Greek god shook his head. "Sorry. I am headed for Olympus, not Iowa. Besides, the Fates, it seems, have chosen you not simply to make the final selection, but to serve as part of the team."

"But why?" Owen practically wailed.

"The Fates alone know that. Perhaps you possess some qualities or some knowledge no one has guessed. Maybe you are simply more open-minded about . . . unusual things than are most mortals."

Owen groaned. "Weird power. Guess it was a pretty dumb idea after all."

"But there is no virtue in questioning it all," Hermes continued with an apologetic smile. "Surely you have read enough mythology to know that one cannot avoid one's fate."

Uneasily he cleared his throat. "But I can see it is rather unsettling to be so abruptly called away. At least I can give you a communication device." He handed Mandy the wand he had stuck in his waistband. She almost dropped it when she noticed two little snakes curling and wriggling along its length. But at least they seem firmly attached.

"Thanks." Gingerly she slipped it into the pocket of her long orange skirt.

Soon they were all inside, and at a word from the witch, the little wooden door swung shut on the daylight. Mandy and Owen, huddled together and blinking against the dimness, stared about the cottage. It was wildly cluttered. Colorfully painted wooden chairs, tables, cupboards, and shelves were piled high with books and baskets and jars of very odd-looking things. Bunches of herbs and strings of onions and garlic hung in dusty swags from the rafters, while in the center of the room rose a large flat-topped oven with its chimney jutting through the ceiling and its sides inlaid with

70

smooth, brightly colored tiles. Near it on a wooden table sat a color TV set.

The impression of oddness and overcrowding was not reduced by the room's new occupants. Lung Nu had deliberately resumed dragon shape, though she'd kept it to the size of a pony. With a little puff of steam she snorted, stretched luxuriantly, and curled up on a rug by the stove. Siegfried stood at the farthest end of the room, clutching his sword and glaring at her. Coyote was poking his head and paws into various cupboards, while the Horned King found himself a shadowy corner and sat alone, quietly fading in and out of sight.

"What a madhouse," Baba Yaga muttered. "Well, let's get this show on the road." She poked through several jars on a shelf and then taking a handful of powder from one, opened the oven door and threw it in. Doing a hobbling little dance she chanted:

"House, house, get off your duff.
Your usual pace is not enough.
Hurry to the ship from outer space,
And we'll put these heathens in their place."

Slamming the door, she shrugged. "Not one of my best efforts, but what do you expect on the spur of the moment?" Then she hoisted up her skirt, clambered on top of the oven, lay down, and promptly went to sleep.

Already the house was rocking under them. "Just like a California earthquake," Owen said, looking at the bunches of herbs and onions swinging from the rafters. Then came a stomach-squashing surge, as if they were on a rapidly rising elevator. Owen and Mandy stumbled to the window.

Mandy groaned. "I really didn't think this was going to work."

"Me neither. I figured I'd wake up about this time."

Below them, the leafy yellow crowns of a vast birch forest were swiftly dropping away. Shredded clouds drifted between the house and the view. When the clouds broke again, there were more trees below, but these were green and tropical looking, while stone temples and squared-off pyramids rose from among them. Suddenly they both flinched back from the window as a large feathered serpent flew by, its golden feathers blazing like the sun.

Other scenes came and went. Through the clouds they caught glimpses of hot, dry-looking places with temples the same baked color as the ground from which they rose. Next might be a cold, forbidding spot with mountains looming in the mists. The scenes came faster and faster, and always seemed farther and farther below them until suddenly the clouds had thinned to blackness and they were up among the stars.

The two huddled more closely together and stared at the stars. Even they looked odd. Faint bluish lines connected some of them into patterns, and when Mandy blurred her eyes out of focus, the patterns seemed almost like people or animals, figures that moved and rustled slightly as if they were alive. Some stars were connected into two or three overlapping patterns.

"Jeez," Owen whispered. "This isn't the route the space shuttle takes."

"No, and we haven't the same fuel either. Can it really be Chicken Legs running us up here? I mean, there's nothing in space to push against."

"Yeah, but nothing's working in the ordinary way. I mean, we're breathing air in here but there aren't any machines making it, and there're just thin glass windows between us and all that cold vacuum in outer space. We're not going by our rules.''

Mandy nodded. "Right. We're following theirs.''

They looked back at their companions. Coyote was sitting on his haunches eating something grizzly-looking that he'd found in a cupboard. Baba Yaga snored from the top of the stove, while the dragon was curled like a cat at its base. Siegfried had found a whet stone and was sharpening his sword, while in a far, shadowed corner the Horned King sat looking faded and gloomy.

Owen shook his head. "What is this lot going to do once they get there? I mean, I suppose it's real space invaders we're talking about here.''

Mandy nodded. "What we really need is some leader type, like Captain Kirk.''

"Or Captain Picard," Baba Yaga, suddenly awake, said from the top of the stove. "He's more my type, more mature. Pity they weren't asked along.''

"Ah, we will do just fine as we are," Coyote said, rubbing the crumbs and grease from his muzzle onto a rug. "But it is time we did a little planning. Okay, everybody, listen up!''

He gave the dragon a nudging kick in her black scaly side. Hissing an angry cloud of steam, she opened her golden eyes. "Beware, dog, or you could become a three-legged deity.''

"I warned you it is not safe to harbor a dragon," Siegfried said, stalking over.

"Stow it, everyone!" Coyote snapped. "We have some serious planning to do. Now, does anyone have suggestions about what we do when we reach this spaceship?''

Siegfried thrust his sword upward, accidentally slicing

through a string of onions and sending the white globes bouncing about the cottage. "All is as clear as crystal! We board the ship and start killing everything in sight!"

"Oh, subtle, subtle," Lung Nu said languidly.

"We could try that, I suppose," Coyote admitted. "Except that we do not know how their weapons measure up against our powers. But in any case, we first have to get on board. And they do not sound like folks who would welcome just any passing chicken house."

"So what do you suggest, puppy?" Baba Yaga said.

"Trickery, of course. The way I see it, we need to fool them into thinking that Earth is very powerful and ought to be left alone. If they actually reach Earth and see what humanity is really like, we are doomed."

"So from the depths of your vast desert-born wisdom," the dragon said, stretching and examining her claws in the flickering stove light, "how do you suggest we manage that?"

"I'm working on it."

"Excuse me if I do not wait up for this revelation." Closing her eyes, she nestled closer to the fire.

The others drifted back to what they'd been doing, except Coyote, who sat gazing out another window, obviously deep in thought. The Horned King looked even glummer and faded from sight for minutes at a time. He was beginning to get on Mandy's nerves. Finally she couldn't stand it any longer and walked up to Coyote.

"Hey, Coyote," she said, scarcely self-conscious anymore about speaking with what looked like a dog, "what is it with the horned guy in the corner? He's not even here half the time, and when he is, he's the spirit of gloom. They didn't say much about him in that book I read."

Coyote blinked, turning away from his starry window.

"Probably because folks don't know a lot about him or don't want to know. I suspect his problem is that he doesn't really belong in any one place. By nature he's a huntsman, always seeking, never finding. He is constantly drifting between realities, moving back and forth between worlds —between your world and his Otherworld, between the land of the living and the land of the dead. He has his spectral hounds and a pack of dead huntsmen, but you wouldn't say he is really a companionable sort."

Mandy shivered. "He gives me the creeps."

"Yep, but that's his job. Spreading fear—fear of death, and of worse—fear of emptiness, of nonbelonging." Coyote flashed his toothy grin. "He is also skilled at carrying off the unwary to strange places."

Owen, who'd been listening, suddenly yelped. Mandy looked at him. "What's the matter?"

Reaching gingerly into his pocket, he slowly pulled out his toy tribble. "It's acting funny. It's purring and wiggling, and I haven't even flipped on the switch."

Mandy looked closer. Sure enough, a pleasant purring was rising from the ball of fur, and it was wriggling in Owen's hand. Owen put it down on the floorboards, and it started inching forward, then sideways, making soft sniffing sounds.

From the top of her stove, Baba Yaga cackled with delight. "Thought it would get around to that. Poor thing must be hungry." She jumped down, rummaged in some sacks and jars, then spread a handful of nuts and dried berries over the boards. Eagerly the golden fur ball wriggled forward, scarfing up the scattered food like a vacuum cleaner.

Owen just stood staring at it. Then finally he said, "Are you trying to say my tribble's come alive?"

"Well, it was bound to, wasn't it?" Baba Yaga snapped impatiently. "I mean, bringing a mythological creature into an atmosphere like this—what did you expect?"

"I'm not complaining," Owen said, squatting down and stroking the creature's fur. It trilled contentedly. He and Mandy spent the rest of the trip playing with the tribble.

At one point, Mandy stood up to stretch her legs and glanced out a window. She thought she could never get tired of looking at those stars. This far from Earth they had lost their faint blue patterns and were just bright jewels set in the deepest black.

Now, however, she stared harder and stepped closer to the window, pushing up her glasses. There was something else out there. Something shaped like a football. A very, very big one.

"Coyote," she said in a trembling voice, "have you figured out a plan yet?"

"I'm working on it," he said from his window on the other side of the house.

"Well, you better work overtime because I think we're there."

Instantly everyone crowded around the two windows on that side. Even the Horned King got up and peered over the others' heads.

"So, that's the spaceship they thought was a comet," Owen said. "Must have thought it was a big comet."

"It *is* a little off scale," Coyote admitted.

"Enormous," the dragon said.

Mandy frowned. "What was it that Han Solo kept saying in *Star Wars*?"

" 'I've got a bad feeling about this,' " Baba Yaga answered.

Owen and Mandy both nodded. "Exactly."

CHAPTER TEN

BOARDING PARTY

Outside, beyond the squares of rippled glass in the cottage windows, the view was of vast blackness, studded with cold, steadily burning stars. Among them hung the huge football-shaped ship. Its surface wasn't really as smooth as a football, Mandy realized as she studied it. It was bristling with stuff. Knobs and projections, disks and towers. Most as big as several city blocks. She hadn't any idea what they did, except that a fair number were very likely weapons.

"Well, it appears that we have arrived," the dragon said. "Now what?"

Coyote stared at their quarry, his front paws resting on the sill. "The first thing we should do is . . . duck!" He hurled himself onto the floor and threw his paws over his face. The others did the same just as the blackness outside flared into light, blinding white light.

The house jerked and began spinning wildly. Furniture toppled, and jars, books, and boxes shot off shelves. The only person who wasn't flat on the floor was Baba Yaga, who was hopping about like an electrified flea, chanting frantically. Then, dropping to her hands and knees, she rooted through the things that were spilled onto the floor until she found a little enameled box. Wrenching open the lid, then the oven, she tossed a pinch of powder into the fire. The house slowed and stopped like a toy winding down.

As Owen staggered dizzily to his feet, Mandy shrieked, "Don't anybody move! My glasses flew off somewhere." Everyone started looking carefully where they stepped, as Mandy crawled around patting the floor. For a moment she thought she'd found them in a puddle of spilled soup, but it was just the remote control for Baba Yaga's TV. Absently she was wiping it off on her skirt when the Horned King pulled her glasses from a pile of spilled firewood and handed them to her. She tried to smile back her thanks without actually looking at him, though she didn't know why. He certainly couldn't sweep her off to any worse place.

Owen was staring out the window. "Hey, that's neat. Did you do that, Baba Yaga?" As Mandy joined him at the window, he added, "Doesn't look like much protection, though."

Looking out the window now was like being inside a soap bubble. A thin rainbow film seemed to surround the house. Baba Yaga snorted and started stuffing things back onto shelves. "Since when does magic have to look impressive to work? It's a protection spell, and a good one too."

As if to prove this, another blast of light shot from the huge ship, but now the house only bobbed around gently like a bubble on a pond. Two more blasts followed with the same effect.

"Oh, excellently done, witch!" Siegfried exclaimed. "Now, can you hurl back some magic and fry them to a crisp?"

"Look," she snapped while still trying to tidy the cottage, "if you had wanted an attack-class enchanter, you should have hired Merlin or someone. I'm just a witch. Spells and personal enchantments, that's my bag. Period."

"Oh, no, you did just fine," Coyote said. "Now the question is how do we get aboard that thing? They don't seem too hospitable. Anybody good at invisibility spells?"

There was total silence. Then Siegfried said, "Invisibility? Well, I have the Tarnhelm, of course." He reached into a cloth bag hanging at his waist and pulled out a wad of—nothing. Then he went through motions as if putting on a hooded cloak and suddenly disappeared.

His voice came from the same spot. "Unfortunately it is only large enough for one."

"Well, I can fix that," Baba Yaga said. Kicking amid the debris on the floor, she finally pounced on what looked like a perfume spray bottle and began spritzing in the direction of Siegfried's voice.

Pretty soon one whole end of the room began billowing with invisibility. Rising and falling clouds of nothing started getting between everyone's vision at that end of the cottage. In a moment, Siegfried came struggling out of it until at last all of him could be seen.

"Vile witch, what have you done to my magic cape?" he demanded. "It's . . . it's as big as a tent!"

"As big as a cottage, I hope," Baba Yaga said, gathering up the yards and yards of invisibility, bits and pieces of her seeming to disappear as she did so. Then pushing open a window, she shoved the whole thing outside, chanting all the while.

"Hold! That is mine!" Siegfried protested.

"Relax, kid. I just told it to wrap itself around the cottage, leaving running room for the chicken legs, of course."

"Aha!" Coyote exclaimed suddenly. "A couple of simple magic spells. Child's play! But these aliens won't know that, will they? If they are truly devoid of spirit, they probably do not even know that magic exists. They may think we have some sort of fancy technology. Now we need to send them a really intimidating message."

"Hey, this is a house, remember?" Baba Yaga said. "You think I've got a whole bank of communication equipment like Lieutenant Uhura's on the *Enterprise*?"

"Hmm. That is a problem, all right," Coyote said.

"Not really, puppy," the dragon yawned. "I recall that flighty Greek fellow left us a message-sending wand."

With a start, Mandy reached into one of the deep pockets in her skirt. "You mean this?" She held the rod by its tip, keeping her fingers as far as possible from the two writhing snakes.

"Perfect!" Coyote reached for it, realized his paws wouldn't do too well, and in a blur switched into his human shape. Soon the buckskin-clad Indian was sitting cross-legged on the floor holding Hermes' wand in front of his mouth like a microphone.

"Attention, alien ship," he said in a harsh, authoritative voice. "You have entered the territorial space of the planet Earth. Your attack on our ambassadorial shuttle has shown unfriendly intentions, but we have refrained from annihilating you with our superior weapons in order to give you an opportunity to explain and apologize."

There was a long silence in which Coyote cocked his head as if he were still in animal form, listening. Then the wand crackled, and a deep, floppy voice said, "Who are you?"

Coyote winked at his companions. "We are an official delegation from Earth sent to inform you that, for your sake, your plans to invade our planet are ill-advised."

Again long silence. Then, "We offer you safe conduct to come on board and discuss matters."

Coyote put his hand over the wand and whispered to the others, "Should we?"

"It is a treacherous trap!" Siegfried cried. "Just blast them out of the sky."

The dragon's tail delivered a sharp slap to his ankle. "Idiot. We cannot do that. This is bluff, remember? We simply must convince them we *could* blast them out of the sky if we chose."

"Then we had better get on with it, had we not?" Siegfried replied. "Only cowards would turn from a challenge like that."

Coyote looked around at the others. No one objected. Baba Yaga shrugged. "Might as well. But get them to tell you where to go, so I can tell the house. She gets kind of skittish with all this machinery about."

Coyote uncovered the wand. "We will accept your invitation. How are we to board?"

Crackle. Fizz. "A flashing blue light will indicate the landing bay."

Baba Yaga went to the stove and began whispering instructions while Coyote returned the wand to Mandy and shrank back into animal shape. "More comfortable," he said.

Then shaking himself, he assumed a dignified air. "All right, crew, the future of our worlds, mortal and Other, depends on us. Look as intimidating as you can, and leave the talking to me."

There was a sharp jolt, and Owen realized the chicken legs were in action again. "Good thing we're invisible," he whispered to Mandy. "Somehow I don't think we look too intimidating."

They were moving now toward a blue light flashing on

81

the underside of the ship. The closer they came, the more huge and complex the vessel seemed to be. The beacon was flashing above a long gash in the ship's side, which appeared to be the entrance to an enormous hangar. Wearing frozen expressions, they watched as the sides closed in on them. With a shudder, they came to a stop. From outside came the sound of bird claws scratching on a metal deck.

With a thunderous growl, Siegfried unsheathed his sword. "Let the battle lust be kindled, let the enemy quail before our fury! Charge!" Bursting out of the door, he leaped onto the deck and began fumbling and fighting with the enveloping folds of invisibility.

Clucking disapproval, Baba Yaga followed him down, grabbed up a corner of the cape, and, muttering a shrinking spell, began bunching it up until it was small enough to hand back to Siegfried. Miffed, the Norseman stuffed the cloak away, then strode off with the others following.

Mandy cast an eye over their party. They were not unimpressive. Lung Nu had resumed her full dragon size, and the Horned King was mounted again on his black horse. The tribble, which Owen was carrying, hardly looked very frightening, but at least it was more impressive than her own empty hands. She fumbled in the skirt pocket that didn't hold the snake wand, but all she came up with was an audiocassette she'd meant to play for Owen, and Baba Yaga's TV remote, which she'd slipped in by accident. This last might look a little like a weapon, she decided, if she gripped it threateningly enough.

As soon as they were all assembled, Baba Yaga turned back to her cottage and chanted:

"House, only let in those who came out.
Anyone else you're to throw on their snout."

Turning back around she drew in a sharp breath and added, "Or whatever. Doesn't look like these guys have snouts."

The others followed her gaze. Through a wide-arched doorway, a group of aliens was approaching, crossing the wide stretch of metallic floor in little, bobbing hops.

Staring, Mandy and Owen stepped closer to each other. No matter how gruesome, aliens weren't so bad as long as they were done by special effects. These weren't.

They were all about four feet high and cylindrical, shaped like garbage cans. Their skin looked like rather moldy greenish leather. Each had a circle of long flaps around its middle and another beneath it, which seemed to serve as feet. Around the top of each cylinder was a band of dark blue and orange patches. On the foremost alien, one of these orange patches began vibrating, and a voice spoke in very blubbery-sounding English.

"You will come with us to the council chambers."

All the little leathery feet reversed the direction of their flapping, and without turning, the troop of garbage cans moved back in the direction from which they'd come. The party from Earth looked at each other, shrugged, and followed.

They crossed a wide open plaza with a ceiling like a huge waffle, then turned into what was the first of long, mazelike routes of corridors, ramps, and moving sidewalks. They hadn't progressed far, however, before Baba Yaga stopped, muttered something about hospitality and arthritic old women, and gave a piercing whistle back down the corridor. In moments, her outsized mortar and pestle came zooming down the hallway, and she climbed in.

All along their route, clusters of aliens gathered and stared. At least, Mandy assumed they were staring. "Too bad they haven't got regular faces," she whispered to Owen. "I'd love to read their expressions."

"I bet there's not another like it in the whole universe," Owen said surveying their party. At its front, Siegfried strode along, gleaming sword in hand, with Coyote trotting confidently at his side. Behind them, a large space in the procession was taken up by the full-sized dragon, her scales gleaming like black glass and her long tail sweeping arrogantly back and forth.

The clack of dragon claws on the floor was followed by the big thumps and little thumps of Baba Yaga poling herself along in her mortar and pestle. Feeling highly insignificant, the two children came next, but they were followed by the fearful dignity of the dark huntsman. Beneath his awesomely spreading antlers, his eyes glowed as brightly as the sparks struck from the hooves of his great black horse.

At long last, a corridor opened into an immense chamber, its high ceiling glowing with pinkish light. The floor of the vast room was crisscrossed with ridges of different heights and angles, like gym bleachers crazily arranged. Standing along the ridges were thousands and thousands of garbage cans, some taller than others but all the same greenish brown. Mandy thought suddenly of billowing waves of stagnant water.

"If this is their *representative* council," Coyote whispered to no one in particular, "how many millions of these characters are there on this ship?"

When they first entered the chamber, the air was full of a chugging, throbbing sound, but now it bubbled down to silence, and one large garbage can flapped toward them down a broad ramp.

One of its orange patches shivered, and in fat, chewy English it said, "We were unaware that you people possessed the technology to send a ship to intercept us, particularly one with such sophisticated defenses. It is, of course, nothing compared to our abilities, but we respect technology so we grant you this audience.''

Coyote trotted forward and sat down on his haunches. ''Most kind of you, honorable sir, but in truth it is *we* who are granting *you* this audience. When at first we received your pathetic little message on our planet, it did not seem worth our bother. But more humane sentiments prevailed, and this delegation has been dispatched to warn you of your folly. There is still time for you to save yourselves and go elsewhere.''

''These are meaningless words, odd-looking person. Our distant scanning of your planet detects no technological threat to us.''

''Bah! You have been deluded by your own machines. Our technology is of an order too advanced, too grand for you even to comprehend. Tell me, did your distant scanning report intelligent species in the variety you see before you?''

For a moment, the spokesman garbage can warbled to an associate, then replied, ''No. Most looked like that tall one behind you or the two short ones in the middle. Such diversity is disturbing but of little account as long as you are controllable enough to use as slaves. Our concern at present is whether or not you possess sufficient weapons technology to resist us. Our studies indicate that clearly you do not, so our attack will proceed.''

Gravely Coyote shook his head. ''Ah, what a great pity to see such a fine species as yours destroy itself like this. We are now a rather peaceful people, keeping ourselves to ourselves, but not long ago there was terrible warfare between ourselves and the civilizations on the other eight planets of this Solar System. And it is we who defeated every one of them.''

Again there was consultation among the garbage cans.

"You lie. All those other planets have no civilizations. Our scanners show they are lifeless."

"There, you see? What more proof do you need?"

A moment of stunned silence, then obviously troubled conversation broke out among the huge assembly. Mandy felt like running forward and hugging Coyote, but just then she noticed a group of shorter, more footstool-shaped aliens hopping up toward the big one. They talked quickly with much waving of their leather flaps, and some held devices up to the spokesman's blue patches.

Flopping closer to them now, that creature spluttered, "You are liars! Our scanners have shown that even your ship contains no advanced technology beyond a single vision-receiving device. How it is propelled and shielded we have not yet determined, but clearly no significant technology is involved. Why, even now you have dared to come among us with no sophisticated technology of any kind other than the meager device held by that pale, short person."

Mandy looked down at the TV remote in her hand and felt particularly foolish.

"Whatever powers you possess," the creature continued, "they are clearly no threat to us."

It garbled out something to a cluster of tall garbage cans by the door, and this group hopped forward, clutching long metal rods in their flaps. The poles were raised and a blazing network of light shot between them, trapping the group from Earth in a sizzling network of energy.

As they all crowded in to avoid the stinging web, Baba Yaga hunched down in her mortar and snarled, "I've got a real bad feeling about this too."

CHAPTER ELEVEN

BREAKOUT

For a while they fought. Siegfried slashed at the net with his sword, and Lung Nu shrank to her human form and fought at his side. But it proved useless, and soon they were hauled off like so many netted fish to a small, featureless room and confined there.

Sitting with the others on the floor, Mandy looked up and thought they all looked about as gloomy as the Horned King. Then she stood up and stared carefully around. "Hey, where *is* the Horned King?"

Siegfried glanced up dully. "I have seen nothing of him since those villainous creatures threw their cowardly net over us."

"You don't suppose it could have hurt him, do you?" she said in a worried tone. "Short-circuited him or something?"

Coyote sighed and sat up. "No, he probably just bolted to wherever it is he keeps fading in and out to. At least maybe he can warn the others, tell them we have failed. Couldn't ask for a better herald of doom."

"Is technology really so much stronger than magic?" Owen asked.

"Not stronger, really," Coyote said, "but different. They work on different principles. When they confront each other, technology often seems stronger because it is more general and can harness great power very quickly. Magic is very specific. Each one of us here surely has the power to overcome certain specific devices of theirs, but when they channel vast general energy into things like that energy net or the death rays with which this ship is probably equipped, we're helpless. Even if all the Otherworlds united against them, I doubt if we could stop them."

"Perhaps not," Siegfried said, "but are we just going to roll over like beaten dogs and give up without a fight?"

Coyote growled. "I hate to. I hate the thought of those creatures taking over our beautiful Earth. It isn't their looks. I've seen uglier. It's their empty spirits. Creatures with so little imagination they haven't created even one Other-world!"

"But is this not a paradox of logic?" Lung Nu asked. "Is not imagination necessary for any form of advancement?"

"Perhaps stubborn trial and error have the same effect. Unless, of course . . ."

Baba Yaga jumped to her feet. "Will you two stop wallowing in philosophy and think of some way to get us out of here?"

"Old woman, are you so anxious to face those weapons again?" the Dragon Princess said.

"No, but I don't like being pushed around by walking footstools! If I'm going to end my glorious wicked career fried in this tin can, I'd rather do it fighting!"

"Oh, bravely said!" Siegfried exclaimed, jumping up. "At least we can make them remember us."

Lung Nu brushed the silky black hair from her face and looked up at him. "I am loath to admit it, but the Norseman is right. We here are representing some of Earth's most glorious heritage. If we allow ourselves to mope around until they decide to execute us, we are abandoning that trust. At the very least, we can break out of this jail and cause as much trouble as possible before they annihilate us."

Mandy and Owen had been huddled together silently, but now Owen shyly stood up. "Well, we two haven't a shred of magic, but kids are always good at causing trouble. I mean, what's there to lose?"

Mandy smiled at him. "Right. I say, go for it!"

"Okay, okay," Coyote said. "I get the picture. Die for a great cause. Go down in a blaze of glory. Suits me. But how do we get out of here?"

"You're the brains of this outfit," Baba Yaga chortled. "Think of something."

While Coyote sat thinking, Lung Nu and Siegfried tried their magic swords on the wall to no effect. Baba Yaga's opening spells were equally useless on the door. When they sat back down, discouraged, Coyote said, "If this room's intended as a jail, they've probably focused so much technology into securing it that no magic would work here."

Baba Yaga snorted. "If I could just get near one of those leather trash cans, I wouldn't need magic, I'd bash it with my pestle. Good, solid Russian oak."

"Hmm, yes," Coyote said. "Maybe that's it. Let's try a little *simple* technology on them. Siegfried, hand over the Tarnhelm."

"Why is it that everybody gets to use this but me?"

"Because you're a big, brave hero and don't need it as much as puny, sneaking tricksters. Now hurry it up."

Reluctantly Siegfried pulled the wadded invisibility cloak from its bag and handed it to Coyote. The animal flailed around with it until Mandy stepped in to help drape the cloth around him so that everything including his bushy tail tip was well hidden.

"All right, everyone," his muffled voice said from nowhere. "Get ready to gripe about equipment malfunction."

Suddenly a high yipping filled the room, followed by a wailing, piercing howl.

Baba Yaga threw her bony hands over her ears. "Worse than a Siberian wolf, that is. Oh, I get it!"

Vigorously she began pounding on the door. "Hey, out there! Some of your blasted technology's gone wrong in here. Something's wailing like a . . . like a banshee. We don't know beans about these things, but you'd better get in here and fix it. Who knows, maybe it'll make the whole ship explode!"

For long moments the only sound was the piercing howls echoing back and forth in the metal-walled room. Baba Yaga was about to start hammering again when the door hissed open, and two large garbage cans holding weapons waddled in.

Both were suddenly hit by an invisible nothing and rolled onto the floor. In a flash Baba Yaga was using her wooden pestle on them like a golf club, skidding them over the floor so hard they bounced back and forth between the walls.

Siegfried and Lung Nu burst into the corridor and began hacking about with their swords. Against living enemies, it seemed, their enchanted swords and armor were very effective.

Owen and Mandy followed the warriors out just as Siegfried's sword sliced one of the aliens right down the middle. Thick white liquid spurted everywhere. Both looked away only to see Baba Yaga's face turn a sickly green.

"Yuck," she muttered. "Even if these creatures do have

plump children, you won't catch *me* eating any of them. Come on, kids, let's stick with Coyote. ''

A bushy tail tip was disappearing down the corridor. Willingly the two ran after it as Baba Yaga pounded along beside them in her mortar. The tail kept jerking about to the sound of cursing until finally it disappeared altogether and Coyote's human face was staring down at them from the folds of an invisible hood.

"This thing definitely wasn't designed for short, four-legged folk to run in. Where're the others?''

Just then the little Asian warrior and the tall Norse one came loping up, triumphant smiles on their faces. Mandy and Owen tried not to look at the thick white goo dripping from their swords. "I'll never touch marshmallow sauce again,'' Owen muttered.

"Where to now?'' Siegfried said brightly.

"As far from here and as fast as possible,'' Coyote answered. "Then we can think up something more subtle.''

The sound of leathery foot flaps in the distance sent them hurrying after Coyote up a narrow side corridor. He'd thrown back his hood so it looked as if there were a disembodied head floating before them. Several corridors crossed, and the head led them along one, then up a ramp, along several more corridors, and up more ramps. Many times they had to dodge garbage cans, but the fact that these creatures always seemed to travel in groups meant that they made enough noise to give the fugitives warning.

While they were catching their breath at a crossroads, Owen whispered, "I just figured out why it's all ramps and no stairs. Their flappy little feet couldn't handle stairs.''

Mandy nodded. "Well, I can't handle many more ramps. My legs are killing me. Surely we've lost them by now.''

"And ourselves as well," Lung Nu added.

"Well, since we didn't know where we were in the first place," Coyote observed, "we're hardly lost now."

"Deep theoretical thinking," the Dragon Princess said dryly. "Where then, in theory, are you taking us?"

"Anywhere we can cause trouble. Nothing against you warrior types. A little slaughter has its place, but if we're going to go down fighting, we might as well take as much as possible down with us. If we could find some sort of control center or engine room, we could really maximize our damage."

"So why do we have to keep going *up*?" Mandy asked. "Couldn't a control room be *down* just as easily?"

"Sure, maybe. But Coyotes, particularly divine ones, have good hunting instincts, you know. Besides, this thing is sort of ball-shaped. Wouldn't it be logical for controls to be in the center?"

"Sure," Baba Yaga said, "if animated garbage cans have the same ideas of logic. But lead on. The longer we wander around lost, the longer it'll be before someone blasts us into eternity."

"She is almost as cheery as that fellow with the antlers on his head," the princess muttered.

"How can anyone remain gloomy with the promise of battle ahead?" Siegfried said, brandishing his sword. "Onward and upward!"

Coyote rolled his eyes, which Owen thought rather disconcerting in a disembodied head. They continued the climb. As he trudged along endless corridors and tightly spiraled ramps, Owen tried to blank out his mind. If he let a thought slip in, it was usually about how this couldn't be happening, or shouldn't be happening, or at least shouldn't be happening to *him*. All very disheartening, considering that it was.

He was trying so hard not to think that he walked with a grunt into Coyote's invisible back. He blinked, looked around, and realized that he was standing in the open. Really open, like outside. Mandy was standing beside him, pushing her glasses firmly up as if to confirm what she was seeing.

The space above them was vast, a great arching sky of misty blue. But something was wrong. He looked more intensely at the sky and realized that in fact it was the other side of this huge ship. It was as though they had moved inward through the skin of a ball and were now looking through the inflating air at the other part of the inside. He could walk halfway around, Owen realized, though it would probably take him ages, and eventually look back ''up'' at where he was standing now.

The thought suddenly made him so dizzy he felt like throwing himself to the ground and clutching things so he wouldn't drift off into that vast topsy-turvy space. He glanced at Mandy, who looked distinctly pale, but the others seemed unaffected, except by the size.

''Big,'' Siegfried observed.

Baba Yaga whistled, ''Think of all the trash cans that can live in this thing.''

''Look at all the fields,'' Lung Nu said, pointing at the plant-covered ground that stretched off in all directions, gradually sloping up until it met the misty distance overhead. ''What do they need our world for? They have one of their own.''

Coyote snorted. ''Maybe they'd rather have a horizon that curves down rather than up. There isn't even a moon to howl at in here. Though it does look like something's up in the sky.''

The rest squinted up and were able to make out a series of glowing rods floating about in the central space. In the very center, there seemed to be a cluster of cubes, their surfaces reflecting an opalescent rainbow of light.

Owen looked away from the dizzying vault to scan the surrounding fields, endless rows of greenish purple plants with thick, juicy-looking leaves. If these are farms, he thought nervously, there must be farmers. He reached into his pocket to stroke Tribble's comforting fur. "Shouldn't we try to hide or something?"

"Fie! It is cowardly to skulk and hide," Siegfried scolded, "when there is a whole world waiting to be devastated."

"What some people lack in brains, they make up for in confidence," Lung Nu muttered.

"Ah," Baba Yaga chortled, "Eastern fatalism versus Western brashness."

"And both are useless without a plan!" Coyote snapped. "Now, we're not going to have much impact on a place this size if we just go about smiting. We all have certain talents, and they'll be put to best use if we concentrate on certain targets. Those cubes floating in the center up there are obviously important and so, I'd guess, are those buildings or whatever." He pointed to what looked like random piles of cubes rising out of the fields some miles in either direction.

"All right, captain," Baba Yaga said, "give us our assignments and let's get moving. It goes against a witch's grain to die in a *good* cause. If I think about it too long, I might just change my mind and set up business here hawking love potions to the natives."

Coyote looked at her severely. "That wouldn't protect you, once Russia and its culture are destroyed."

"Bah, you uppity dog. Can't you take a joke? Gallows humor, we witches specialize in it. Now, get on with it, will you?"

"Right. I'll keep the Tarnhelm and see what mischief an invisible trickster can get into in that clump of cubes over there. You, witch, take Owen and Tribble in your mortar and try to create some havoc in that other cluster. And since you can fly, princess, I suggest you, Siegfried, and Mandy find something to meddle with in that floating cluster up there."

Immediately Siegfried started complaining about having to rely on a vile worm for transportation, but Lung Nu ignored him, and in a swirl of mist melted and expanded into a dragon form, bigger than any she'd conjured so far.

Mandy and Owen paid the event little attention. They stood looking at each other rather awkwardly. Then hesitantly Mandy grabbed Owen's sweaty hand. "I'm sorry I got you into this. Maybe a club deliberately seeking out weirdness wasn't such a great idea."

"Well, maybe neither were my smart-aleck ideas about the mythology paper."

Mandy tried not to snuffle but did anyway, then quickly forced a smile. "But hey, this has got to be more interesting than just getting zapped by the space invaders' disintegrating ray or being herded into slave camps. In a couple of days that's what'll happen to Tracy Trueblood and her gang. To everyone else too, for that matter. Boring city."

"Right," Owen said with a wobbly grin. "Let's hear it for weird power."

They exchanged a secret *W* handshake.

Just then piercing, sirenlike tooting split the air. It seemed to rise from spots near and far, the closest being a pipe sticking out of a planted field.

"What on earth!" Siegfried exclaimed.

"It isn't," Coyote noted. "And my guess is that it's their 'prisoners have escaped' alarm. Everyone to your posts!'' He shrank down to animal shape, all the while tucking invisibility securely around him.

''Aye, aye, captain,'' Baba Yaga said, leaning over the side of the mortar and cramming Owen in beside her. ''To boldly go where no witch has gone before!''

CHAPTER TEWLVE

COMMANDO TEAM ONE

As the mortar started jolting off over the landscape, Owen wondered which he'd die of first—violent motion sickness or a splitting headache. But gradually Baba Yaga worked things into a smoother rhythm with longer and longer leaps.

Then as they hopped along, she started chanting short, nasty-sounding phrases and occasionally freeing up a hand for quick clawing gestures. Peering over the edge of the mortar, Owen noticed that the plants below them seemed to blacken and wither as they passed. Suddenly he had a vision of the wicked witch in *The Wizard of Oz* planting her field of poison poppies.

In the cramped quarters, he twisted around and looked at Baba Yaga, her face aglow with wicked delight. "Are you doing that to their crops?"

"Yes, isn't it wonderful? A witch's dream. Absolute license to do as much mischief in as short a time as possible."

The sirens had stopped their hooting, and now the only noise Owen heard was the witch's chanting and the regular thump of their vehicle on the ground. He had grown tired of watching the spreading pestilence in their wake, when, turning ahead, he suddenly noticed a large number of garbage cans issuing from a dark opening in the ground. They were carrying metal poles.

"Uh-oh," he said pointing. "They'll get us for sure!"

"Not if we hide, kid."

"Hide? Where? There's nothing around for miles but those rubbery little plants."

"Hey, I'm a witch. Give me a little credit, will you?"

When they next touched ground, Baba Yaga hopped out of the mortar, turned it on its side, and sat down in a furrow between two rows of plants. Doubtfully Owen joined her. "This isn't much of a hiding place. They'll see us for sure."

"Not a chance."

"We're invisible or something?"

"No, I can't do that one. I've made us look like a couple of these nasty little plants."

Owen looked himself and his companion over. "I hate to tell you, but we still look like a boy and an old woman crouching in a field."

"That's because it's a joint spell and you're inside, not outside of it. Now shut your mouth. Even in this place plants don't talk."

Owen did more than shut his mouth. He scrunched down and buried his face in the gritty black dirt. For a long while there was silence—an unnatural, empty silence. No birds or breezes fluttered over these fields. Then came the dry flapping of leather feet, the sound of barrel-shaped bodies pushing their way through rows of low, thick-leaved plants. Owen tried to make himself as small as possible, but he knew it was useless. They'd see him any second now. He hoped they wouldn't take a long time killing him.

Closer now. Very, very close. They must be in the next row. He tensed up for the pain. But none came. The foot flapping and chuggling voices moved off. Farther and farther away. His long-held breath gusted out in a sigh that churned dirt into his face. Cautiously he sat up.

"They've gone," he whispered, scarcely believing it. "They didn't see us."

"Of course not," Baba Yaga snapped, sitting up and brushing grit off her clothes. "I *am* one of the better witches, you know."

When the scout force was some distance down the field, Baba Yaga righted the mortar, and they set off, again, using much lower jumps. They hadn't gone far, however, before they had to go into magical camouflage again. This time they remained upright, disguised as the asparaguslike trees that now surrounded them. Despite their last success, Owen still shut his eyes as low-flying, round ships shot overhead. When he looked again, they were marble-sized balls disappearing over the distant upward-curving fields.

Setting out once more, the two found the piled-up cubes that were their goal now much closer and much larger. Dauntingly large! Owen wondered what good, or rather what bad, they could possibly do in there.

But the prospect of mischief making on this scale had Baba Yaga bouncing with confidence. When they landed near the base of the huge cubes, she surveyed them like a general. "First thing is getting inside. Now, those big, low openings are probably doors, so we'd better stay clear of them. But what about those smaller openings up there? Air shafts, maybe?"

Before Owen could even comment, she had catapulted them to the top of one of the cubes and was examining a pair of square openings about four feet wide. "Bingo!" she said happily. "You can feel air moving in and out. Hang on!"

With a sudden jerk, the mortar hopped into one of the

openings and plummeted down. Owen clutched at the tribble for comfort, and it purred and rippled under his fingers.

With a pop and a jarring thump, they reached the end of the shaft. The mortar had landed upright on the floor of a large, low-ceilinged room. At its far end, a couple of garbage cans stopped what they'd been doing by a bank of instruments and started babbling and hopping toward the intruders.

"Yikes!" Baba Yaga exclaimed, and hastily sent the mortar careering around the corner into a smaller room full of machinery. By the time their two pursuers reached them, they were disguised as another hunk of humming clicking metal. At least, Owen figured, they must be, when the two aliens flapped right by them without a flicker of notice.

When the creatures were out of sight, Baba Yaga moved from her frozen position and chortled, "Now, this looks like someplace to do some first-class sabotage. But for all we know these machines could be what makes their ice-cream toppings. Better look around a bit more and see if we can find something that just *oozes* importance."

Cautiously they hopped out of that room and down several corridors. Owen figured she must have installed some sort of magical muffler, since their usual thumping had become a feathery bump.

Suddenly the corridor they were in ended in openness. Baba Yaga parked the mortar in a darkened side room and disguised it as another of the metal canisters stacked up there. Then they both crept to the end of the corridor and looked out.

The opening led to a metal walkway, a gallery that ran around the walls of a huge cylindrical room. Three glowing columns rose from the floor, some twenty feet below, up to a crisscrossed net of metal beams at least two hundred feet above. Clustered around the base of the columns were devices of every imaginable shape. Several shaped like barbells were pulsing blue and green, while two knobby poles were juggling a steady stream of violet triangles back and forth. There were coils and spheres and various rectangles. Some whirred, others ticked, and a fair number wheezed. One kept shooting yellow lights around a tangle of clear tubing.

"Hey, kid, what do you think?" Baba Yaga whispered excitedly. "Is this important looking or what?"

Owen grinned at her. "Maybe an engine room."

A wicked light gleamed in her eyes. "We sure can have fun here." Then she twitched and stared down the corridor behind them. "Uh-oh, company."

As the sound of feet padded their way, the two saboteurs scurried back to the room where they'd left the mortar. They wedged themselves between canisters, and the witch cast a spell that made them look like one of the crowd.

Waiting in the silence of the darkened room, Owen listened to the patter of approaching feet, which sounded like dozens of small seals. For comfort he reached into his pocket to stroke the tribble. He gave a startled gasp.

"Hush!" Baba Yaga whispered crossly.

Cautiously Owen felt into his pocket again to make sure he was right. He was.

When the footfalls had faded away, the witch turned to him. "Good thing they make such a racket when they walk. What was that yelp about, anyway?"

"My tribble. He's . . . he's . . . tribbles."

"Huh?"

"Two of them. I had one live tribble in my pocket. Now I have two."

Owen reached into his pocket and carefully pulled out

two purring fur balls, one a golden tan, the other a reddish brown.

Slowly Baba Yaga's face crinkled into a smile. "Hee, hee! Let me guess. You had some food in your pocket, right?"

"Sure. I didn't want him to starve. Before I left your cottage, I poured in a whole boxful of crackers. Nothing magical, just commercial crackers."

"Sure, ordinary enough crackers. But what kind of a Trekkie are you? Don't you remember that that's how tribbles reproduce? They eat and eat until they multiply."

"Oh, right. I forgot," Owen said, still struggling with the idea of TV becoming myth, and myth becoming reality. "So that means that if I keep feeding them, I'll get covered over with tribbles the way the *Enterprise* did."

"Sure, I guess. . . ." Suddenly her wizened face lit up. "That's it! That's how we'll sabotage things. Hee, hee! Beautiful!"

"What's it? What's beautiful?"

"Remember what Chief Engineer Scott did at the end of that episode?"

"Well, he . . . he transported all the tribbles to . . . oh, yeah, to the Klingon engine room. But, hey, we only have two tribbles, and I don't want them hurt."

"No, no. We won't use the originals, just the duplicates."

"What duplicates?"

"The ones I'm going to make, of course. You don't think the Sorcerer's Apprentice is the only one who can do that trick, do you? But Mickey Mouse was an amateur. I'm going to make *lots* of duplicates. Come on!"

Gleefully Baba Yaga skittered to the door and peeked out. Then with Owen and his tribbles behind, she tiptoed onto the balcony, and peered into the room below.

"Those garbage cans that tromped by went out here. There must be some way down to the floor level."

Owen looked around too, then pointed to his right. "How about that round, chutelike thing. Maybe they slide down."

"What fun. Yes, that's got to be it. Now I'd better do a double spell. It's stronger, so you'll see it too—on me, at least. But what'll I disguise us as? Oh, of course!"

She muttered something, and suddenly Owen jumped back. He was staring at one of the aliens. "Do I look like that too?"

"Do you look like an ugly leather footstool that's been in the basement too long and gone moldy? Yes, Let's go."

Flapping on ahead of him, the witch/garbage can hopped along the metal walkway until she came to the cutaway tube that slanted to the floor below. After a long hesitation, she jumped into it and slid down, letting out a rather human-sounding squeal. Staggering to her many feet, she waved her fringe of flippers up at him.

Reluctantly Owen sat down. Sliding had never been his playground favorite. Wondering if he looked as funny as she did, he inched forward, let go, and rocketed down to a jarring landing.

Nervously he glanced around. The machinery towering over them looked very alien. In the distance, a clump of garbage cans paid the newcomers no heed.

"Psst! Over here!" Baba Yaga whispered from a sheltered patch where two glowing rectangles met the floor. "Give me the tribbles."

"You won't hurt them?"

"Of course not. My evil specialty is eating children. Just put them down on the floor."

Hesitantly he did. Baba Yaga's flappy alien hands seemed to fumble at her side, but at last she produced a piece of chalk with which she drew a circle around the two fur balls. Then she began chanting and hopping about while her leather hand flaps wriggled like a frenzied hula skirt. Suddenly, instead of two there were four tribbles, then eight, then sixteen. The numbers kept doubling until Owen found himself standing knee-deep in tribbles.

"That's a pretty good starter," the witch said at last. "Come on. Grab Adam and Eve, and let's get another batch going."

Owen took the two original tribbles out of the chalk circle, slipped them back into his pocket, and hurried after the disguised witch. As they continued around the room, he saw the mound of tribbles behind them billowing and spreading like hairy suds. Already they were engulfing the first machine.

"Hey," he whispered urgently. "Won't they be hurt when they get caught in the machinery?"

"No. Yours would be, they're alive. But the duplicates aren't. They'll keep multiplying until there isn't an inch of space in this room or in any crevice of the machines. But they're sort of like Xeroxes, spiritless zombies, you might say."

Owen shuddered. The whole engine room, taken over by zombie tribbles. Talk about weird!

Soon Baba Yaga had found another niche, and her doubling dance was repeated. Once the multiplication was well under way, they moved off to another spot, and then another.

At one point, they passed a pair of real aliens working on a machine. Owen hoped it wasn't the expected thing to exchange polite little greetings. Apparently it wasn't.

Several more batches of tribbles, and they'd worked their way halfway around the room. Then Owen glanced up and saw a dozen garbage cans hopping toward them. They looked armed. The one in the lead stopped and blabbered something at them. Helplessly Owen turned to his companion but couldn't read anything in her expression since she looked like a garbage can to him too.

She said nothing and continued on her way with Owen nervously following. Behind them, the garbage can said something else, and they just walked more quickly. A shout from behind, and the two broke into a run, which sent them moving a lot faster than their flappy-legged disguise would suggest. That's sure blown our cover, Owen thought as he pelted along.

Suddenly the air beside him twanged and exploded with light. "Personal protection time!" Baba Yaga shouted and, with a jab of her hand, set the air around them sparkling. "Stick close!"

They raced around the room with weapon blasts going off around them like fireworks. Suddenly in front of them, another group of aliens was coming their way.

"Trouble," squealed Baba Yaga. "I don't know how many of their weapons it'll take to overload my protective spell."

The oncoming group was also armed, but from the way they were jabbering and pointing, they seemed to be paying more attention to something behind. In the distance Owen could just make out a sort of blurry mass: a fuzzy tide of tribbles that was slowly seeping this way. They'd come almost completely around the engine room.

Beside him, the witch threw back her head and gave a piercing whistle. Now the oncoming garbage cans began yelling, and the ones behind got into firing range again. When Owen and Baba Yaga didn't reply, both groups started firing.

Cowering down under their protective spell, they watched anxiously as it seemed to waver around the edges. Then with a great swishing and thump the mortar was beside them.

Baba Yaga scrambled aboard, yanking Owen after her just as the two waves of garbage cans collided around them. Wielding her pestle like a battle-ax, the witch cleared away some space. Then with a mighty stroke, she jammed the pestle down and sent the mortar arching up into the air to land teetering on the edge of the metal walkway.

Flailing frantically, she tipped them forward onto the solid metal surface and then with another push sent them hopping along it. Weapons fire from below burst around them as they veered into the first corridor opening they saw.

This was not the same route they had taken earlier. It was wider and led through several large rooms, each with its cluster of garbage cans. They weren't bothering with disguises now, only escape. Barreling down corridors and ramps with angry aliens on their trail, Owen was sure they were hopelessly lost, until suddenly they bounded through a wide doorway into open air and the ship's vast artificial daylight.

Explosions of weapons fire continued blossoming around them, but now, free of the low ceilings, Baba Yaga really poured on speed, and the mortar arched into longer, higher leaps. Suddenly, the angry shrieks behind them were drowned out by a renewed and infinitely more raucous wailing from the outside sirens.

"Where to now?" Owen shouted over the noise.

"Don't know. I'm giving our steed its head. Told it to take us somewhere safe. It has good instincts."

As they sped forward, Owen looked up at the artificial sky. The light bars were dimmed behind a thickening overcast. There were even storm clouds at one end. Well, he guessed that was as good a way as any to water the crops.

Then he noticed something else in the sky. Clutching Baba Yaga's arm he pointed. ''I think it's going to take more than instinct to help us now.''

A pair of little round airships were dropping at them out of the clouds, shooting as they came.

Gritting her iron gray teeth, Baba Yaga tried to steer the mortar around flaring bursts. ''Isn't this where the cavalry's supposed to come galloping to the rescue?'' she shouted.

''Depends on which script you're using.''

''With my luck, it's the script for *The Witch's Last Stand*!''

CHAPTER THIRTEEN

COMMANDO TEAM TWO

Mandy watched as Owen and Baba Yaga bounded off in one direction and presumably the invisible Coyote trotted off in another. Beside her, Siegfried and the Dragon Princess were arguing.

Nervously Mandy kept scanning the empty alien fields. They wouldn't be empty for long, she was sure. Any moment there'd be garbage cans hopping toward them, answering the call of the hooting sirens.

Finally she turned to the bearded blond hero. "Come off it, Siegfried. If you want a chance to wield that mighty sword of yours, you're going to have to go somewhere worth attacking. And right now, that means climbing on a dragon's back and flying up to those floating cubes."

"I, a renowned Norse hero, accepting a ride from a dragon? It is outrageous!"

"Right," Mandy shot back. "And where I come from, *outrageous* means terrific, the thing to do." An idea struck her. "Hey, you're not afraid, are you? I bet that's it—you're afraid of heights."

"I afraid? You insult me, you measly mortal. I, Siegfried, the valiant, fear nothing!"

"I don't believe you."

"What, impudent child, you call me a liar too?"

"Nah, just a coward. But, of course, I could be wrong. I'll take it back if I am."

With a powerful leap, Siegfried vaulted to the dragon's scaly back. "There, rash one, you may take it back now."

Mandy smiled. "Oh, I do," she said, trying to scramble up the tail and find a good riding spot of her own. Suddenly she wished she could take the whole thing back. She didn't want to go flying off on the slippery back of a dragon any more than Siegfried did.

The dragon snaked her head around and examined her passengers. "Believe me, it is no pleasure for me to carry the likes of you, Norseman. It is a great blow to my considerable dragonesque dignity. But since I must, I would prefer not to lose you." With a shiver, she ruffled her scales until they rose up around her two passengers like protective saddles.

"Hold on," she called back, "and refrain from tickling!" As the great black dragon lumbered forward, mist began rising around them as if they'd stumbled into a swamp. The mist thickened into a swirling bank of cloud, and suddenly they were airborne. With one hand Mandy grabbed a jutting black scale, and with the other she jammed her glasses more firmly on her face. She started to look down, then stopped herself. Better not think about the hundreds and hundreds of feet already between her and the hard ground.

Really, she thought, with her eyes looking up, it was more like swimming than flying. The dragon, so huge and ponderous on the ground, was as graceful as a fish in the air. Mandy could easily imagine herself as a sea nymph riding a dolphin, its long body undulating smoothly through the water. Below would be bright coral and waving seaweed. She looked, and there was very distant ground.

Gripping the scales, she flung herself forward. It was several trembling minutes before she could open her eyes again. Ahead of her, Siegfried sat stiffly upright. She bet he had his eyes closed too.

Suddenly Mandy realized they were nearing their goal. The cluster of cubes loomed ahead, far bigger than they'd seemed from below. Their pale surfaces reflected rainbow washes of light, while beyond them hung the other side of this sphere, where everything ought to be clinging upside down. The thought made her dizzy again, and she had to jam her eyes shut.

When she opened them once more, the huge cubes were filling all of her sight. Now she wasn't dizzy, just awed.

White clouds billowed more thickly around them, and Lung Nu seemed to settle herself like a cat on a pillow. She looked around at her passengers.

"Comfortable?"

"Perfectly," Siegfried said in an icy tone.

"Me too," Mandy said, grateful for the obscuring clouds. "But what do we do now?"

"Well," the dragon replied, "one might assume that since it is located in the center of their world, this is the place from which they control their environment. After all, they must make air and light and probably have rain or some way to water the crops. So, for a nature spirit, this seems just the right sort of place to cause trouble."

"Just land on it, worm," Siegfried said coldly, "and I will find some trouble of my own, I guarantee you."

"Yes, I am sure you will," Lung Nu said as she rolled

herself and her cloud to the right. "I think there is an opening ahead."

As the dragon glided around the floating cubes, they found one square with an open face. It was hollow inside, like a waiting aircraft hangar. With a smooth ripple, the dragon swooped in.

Several garbage cans were puttering around a circular airship. They shouted, jumped about, and began firing weapons. Mandy crouched down hoping the dragon had some sort of protective magic, but Siegfried jumped off and charged toward the enemy, waving his enchanted sword.

Then in a cloud of steam, Mandy felt her mount shrinking beneath her. Hastily she jumped off and soon found herself standing beside Lung Nu in her human form. The princess grabbed her arm and dragged her through an open doorway.

"We will let the invincible hero handle defense while we find some tampering to do."

"Will he be all right?" Mandy asked, looking back through a doorway lit up with energy blasts.

The little woman smiled. "Oh, that trusty magical sword he's always bragging about ought to be a match for little hand weapons like that."

Together they ran down a long, narrow corridor and suddenly found themselves in a room lined with what looked like computer consoles. Staring around, Mandy couldn't make any sense of the dials and glowing displays, and from the frown on Lung Nu's face, it seemed the princess couldn't either.

Shrugging, Lung Nu said, "I have not the slightest idea of how computers work. I will just have to rely on instinct." Eyes closed, she walked slowly around the consoles, hands slightly outstretched, with a look of intense concentration on her face. Then her lips softened into a smile as if she were meeting an old friend. Confidently she walked forward and placed her hands on a set of controls.

"Rain. This portion controls precipitation. Of course, they are such orderly sorts here, they never let it get out of hand. No thunderstorms, no snow. But with a little encouragement, to say nothing of enchantment . . ."

Mandy waited tensely, but the machine didn't blow up under her companion's attention, so she looked around for something she could do. She felt profoundly useless. She hadn't an ounce of magic and wasn't much good with computers, even those on Earth. The technology she was toting around in her pockets wasn't of much use either. The snaky wand she definitely didn't want anything to do with, and the audiocassette tape was about as useless as things came.

What about the TV remote, though? She pulled it out, remembering how one of her classmates used to say that his TV remote could open all his neighbors' garage doors. Could it mess anything up here, she wondered?

Standing like a cop on TV, she gripped the remote in both hands, aimed it at the computer, and began pressing buttons. ON, OFF, VOLUME, CONTRAST, MUTE, and all the channel selectors.

Nothing whatever happened.

The noise behind her, however, suddenly increased. She turned and saw Siegfried backing down the corridor, swinging his sword in blinding arcs before him. A half dozen garbage cans were advancing on him, firing their weapons.

He stumbled into the room. "Run! I don't know how long my powers can hold them off!"

Mandy threw a panicky glance at Lung Nu, but the Dragon Princess was still communing with the computer. And where was there to run anyway? The room didn't seem to have any other exit.

112

Shrugging, she resumed her TV-cop stance. Might as well go down looking as if she were fighting. Boldly she pressed the big, unmarked red button.

One of the energy bolts zapping toward Siegfried suddenly stopped in midair. The garbage can seemed to look at its weapon, shake it, then run in retreat.

Mandy stared at her own "weapon." Surely this hadn't done that. Experimentally she aimed it at another of the aliens firing at Siegfried. She pressed the red button and again an enemy energy bolt fizzled in midair. Moments later, that alien fled.

Some TV remote, Mandy thought. But then it *had* belonged to a witch. Maybe Baba Yaga used the red button to meddle in the TV shows she watched. Happy now, Mandy fired again and again until the little guys harassing Siegfried had all fled.

He turned and looked at her. "You amaze me, mortal. You have definite hero possibilities. But come, we must flee. They'll only bring reinforcements."

He charged toward Lung Nu just as she was lowering her hands from the computer. Looking a little befuddled, the princess allowed herself to be dragged off while Mandy followed, feeling suddenly like an important rear guard.

Siegfried headed right toward one of the walls and, with a slash of his sword, split open the metal panel. As she followed the others through, Mandy stared at the ragged opening. She guessed the walls were thin up here so this place could float.

The next room was empty, but the one beyond that was filled with more computers. Lung Nu rushed toward them, but as the other two followed, a large contingent of armed garbage cans came bouncing into the empty room. Yelling fiercely, Siegfried leaped among them, swinging his sword and hacking off bits and pieces of the enemy. Desperately

Mandy began firing her weapon, working the red button even faster as some of the aliens turned their weapons at her.

At last, however, the group was too chopped up and disarmed to continue fighting and shuffled back into a corridor, leaving Mandy and Siegfried to race for the adjacent room.

Lung Nu was standing there, shaking her head at the rows of gleaming alien computers. "I can't do much with this one. It controls light, not one of my fields. But I could, what's the term, short-circuit it. One of you cry for me."

"Cry?" Siegfried said indignantly.

"Yes, you know, with tears."

"Heroes never cry!"

"I doubt that. Well, mortal children do. Cry, Mandy."

"I . . . I can't."

"Try. Dragons cannot cry, and I need tears."

"But . . . I'm not sad exactly. Scared, yes, but . . ."

"Well, become sad. Think of your dog dying horribly when the aliens attack Earth."

"I don't have a dog."

"Well your best friend, then, or a baby brother—anything."

"Well, I've got them, but I just can't cry on cue. Yow!" Tears welled up in her eyes as pain shot from the foot Siegfried had just stomped on.

"Direct action is better than sentiment," he said smugly.

"Thank you," Lung Nu said as she quickly brushed a finger against Mandy's damp cheek. Crouching down, she smeared her finger over the floor, then blew gently on the spot. Soon the smudge of dampness grew to a puddle and then to a pool. The Dragon Princess stood in its midst, swaying like a willow and singing a low, liquid melody. The water kept rising and rising.

Mandy watched as it climbed higher among the winking, humming bank of computers. Suddenly she yelled in alarm, "Hey, we don't want to be standing in this when the water triggers something. We could get electrocuted."

Wading through the knee-high water, she grabbed the swaying princess and pulled her toward a ramp rising to a far door. "You too, Siegfried," she yelled. "Who knows how many volts a Norse hero can take."

They came close to finding out. Siegfried had just grabbed the edge of the ramp and swung clear of the rising water when something cracked and exploded behind them. In seconds the whole room was hissing and booming with jagged light. Then everything went dark. Yelling gustily, Siegfried hung on the edge of the ramp and used his sword to gash a hole low in the room's wall. The rising torrents gushed into the next room and began pouring toward another set of computers.

The three now hurried up the ramp, Mandy's long skirt flapping wetly against her ankles. "Good work, you two," she said. "Now can we cut out of here?"

Siegfried scowled. "What? When there are still enemy left standing?"

Mandy groaned. "Hey, this whole spaceship is full of standing enemy. But if we hang around here, we're going to get ganged up on until even your magic won't hold out."

"The girl is right," Lung Nu said. "The longer we use brains instead of"—she stopped and smiled almost apologetically—"*as well* as brawn, the longer we will last."

"Then let us find an exit," the Norseman said, charging down a corridor.

The rooms and halls they passed through were very dark except for the winking lights on occasional clusters of computers. Lung Nu stopped at one to see if there was anything she could do to it, but then stepped back and shook her head. "No, this one is audio. Orders to the populace, alarms, mood music for the workplace. Not my field."

As the woman moved on to the next one, Mandy looked about nervously. Surely they'd caused enough trouble here already.

"Ah," the princess said dreamily, "temperature. I can deal with temperature." She leaned forward and had just closed her eyes when a large troop of garbage cans bobbed into the far end of the room.

"Forget the temperature controls," Siegfried said firmly. "It is becoming hot enough here already."

Lung Nu looked up, cursed in Chinese, and pulled out her own curved sword. Resolutely, she took a stand beside Siegfried. Then with a joint yell, they charged off toward the garbage cans.

Hastily Mandy reached into her pocket for the TV remote and instead pulled out the audio tape. Annoyed she dropped that into her other pocket and fumbled again for the remote.

Suddenly she was nearly knocked off her feet. The most piercingly awesome sound was blasting out of her pocket—the pocket with Hermes' wand and the cassette tape. Her favorite rock group, the Screeching Screamers, was now blaring out of it at top decibels. Hermes' messenger wand was acting like a super boom box.

Nearly deafened, Mandy grabbed the two and was about to hurl them away from her. Then she paused. Ducking behind the heat computer, she sped back toward the computer bank they had just passed. From the other side she could hear swords hacking and alien weapons sizzling.

With the horrible sound throbbing in her pocket, she skidded to a halt and stared at the sound computer. Unlike Lung Nu, she had no magical instincts to tell her what to do.

Dropping to her knees, she prayed desperately to the God she knew from church, and then to every mythical being she'd ever heard about, throwing in Elvis at the end, for good measure.

She stood up, saw a slot in the side of the machine, and tossed the wand and the tape into it.

Instantly the room shook with noise. No rock concert had ever topped this. Throwing her hands over her ears, Mandy stumbled out from behind the computer to see the remaining garbage cans in panicky retreat, with Lung Nu and Siegfried crouched on the floor, arms flung over their heads.

"Let's get out of here!" Mandy bellowed at them.

Siegfried stood up, a look of intense pain on his face. Then he nodded and, grabbing up his sword, plunged it into the wall. Cold wind gushed through.

Beyond the torn wall was sky, darkened threatening sky. The floating light rods had dimmed to the wattage of a pale moon, and at the far end of the ship's great interior space, storm clouds were piling into billowing heaps.

Mandy turned to yell something at Lung Nu, only to see her little armor-clad form swelling and changing into the shape of a dragon. "Climb aboard!" the princess called. "It promises to be a wild night ride ahead." Then, laughing, she lowered her dark dragon face to the Norseman. "Siegfried, dear, how about singing the 'Ride of the Valkyrie' for effect?"

In moments, the two passengers were seated on the scaly back. Beneath them, muscles rippled and bunched and then the dragon plunged into the turbulent air. Mandy was glad of the darkness—less dizzying reality to see. The wind of their flight whipped back Siegfried's powerful voice as he sang a wild, wordless tune.

Suddenly there was more illumination about than came

from the dim floating rods and the distant lightning. A formation of glowing balls was swooping toward them like the bad-guy blips in a computer game.

Considering the numbers, it no longer looked like a winning game.

CHAPTER FOURTEEN

IN A BLAZE OF GLORY

Mandy gripped her glasses with one hand and the black scales with the other as the dragon swooped through stomach-churning acrobatics, then shot to where the storm clouds were building into a dark, boiling mass.

Timidly she opened her eyes. The clouds into which they dived were hurling lightning bolts back and forth, and the wind that rushed past was cold and filled with the sharp scent of lightning-sizzled air. Carefully Mandy looked behind them.

Glowing tennis balls had followed them into the clouds. The dragon dived just as one ship shot out a weapons beam. Another beam caught them square on, but the deadly energy only splattered over them like sparks hitting glass. Mandy flinched against the light, wondering how long the dragon's protective enchantment would hold. With a deafening crack, lightning shot out of a cloud and pierced one of the pursuing ships. Before the explosion finished flowering, a second ship met the same end.

Veering upward, the dragon shot into a dark bank of

119

clouds. Several ships followed, their weapon blasts filling the clouds with hellish light. Then in a blinding flare of lightning, three more ships vanished.

Looping downward, the dragon lost their last pursuer to a wave of sheet lightning. Mandy huddled close against the dragon's back thinking that no, it was definitely not wise to mess with a storm goddess, not in the middle of a thunderstorm.

As in old war movies, they dropped in a steep dive toward the ground, then pulled up to skim low over the fields. From the regularly placed alarm tubes below came the amplified sounds of the Screeching Screamers. Right on, Mandy thought gleefully, wondering if it was blasting through all the outer layers of the ship as well.

In the fields ahead of them, they were coming up on two clusters of piled-up cubes, some miles apart. Angling upward, the dragon now circled around surveying the scene. A large number of garbage cans seemed to be issuing from one of the clusters in pursuit, apparently, of a single hopping object. From another direction a half dozen glowing tennis balls shot in, firing their weapons at the same target.

For a moment, the dragon hovered above the battle, then like a hunting hawk she dived downward. Singling out one ship, she matched its speed, then swooped on top of it, clutching the thing between her four clawed feet. It jerked and bucked but could not dislodge her. Lowering her head, she stared into the little ship's view port, opened her mouth in a many-toothed grin and began breathing fire over it. When she finally let go, it dropped powerless to the ground in a very rough landing.

One of the remaining ships now shot up toward the dragon, but instead of trying to evade it, she shot directly at it, breathing fire like a welder's torch. Mandy could feel the heat rising through the scales, but never quite saw what happened to the ship, because when the smoke cleared, it was gone. The last four ships hesitated a moment then darted away.

The dragon dropped lower now, and Mandy could see that the object below was definitely Baba Yaga's mortar. Squinting, she had just made out Owen when suddenly parts of the mortar began to vanish and reappear.

"The Tarnhelm!" Siegfried exclaimed in front of her. "That wild dog must have joined them."

They were nearly on top of them now, though the dragon's attempts to match the mortar's jolting pace almost made Mandy airsick for the first time that day.

"Greetings," the dragon called, and in the cramped mortar three oddly matched faces stared up at them. "Want a lift?"

"Not on your life!" Baba Yaga yelled back. "I've given the mortar its head, and it's leading us back to the cottage. This little baby's better than a homing pigeon."

Suddenly the word "home" sounded very good to Mandy, for all that it also sounded unattainable. It must have affected Siegfried the same way, she realized, for he waved his sword in the air and shouted, "Follow that mortar!"

Like a hovering cloud, the dragon did, but soon Mandy was having difficulty seeing the others because of the fog. That was a surprise, until she realized the dragon must have conjured it to help conceal them.

Despite the damp, cloaking grayness, they could follow the others by the regular thumping as the mortar landed, but suddenly there were three startled yells and the thumps stopped. Dropping lower, the dragon circled back. Using a sleeve to wipe the fog from her glasses, Mandy rammed them back on and scanned the ground. Fleetingly through the mists, she saw the dark opening of a downward ramp. The others must have stumbled into it accidentally in the fog.

"Hold on!" Lung Nu shouted over her shoulder. In seconds they'd dropped out of the fog and were shooting down a wide, steeply sloping passage. Mandy suddenly realized that Siegfried was sitting a lot closer to her then he had been before. The dragon must have shrunk her size. Even so, the walls and ceiling of the passage whipped by uncomfortably close to her head. Mandy wished she could make herself smaller too. But at least they were flying. From the scraping noise far ahead of them, it sounded as if the mortar was tobogganing down.

Abruptly swooping up, they were suddenly skimming through open space to make a rather shaky landing on the hard metal deck. "Everyone dismount," Lung Nu said weakly. "The smaller I am, the heavier you are."

Siegfried swung down with dignity, but Mandy leaped off and ran back to where the mortar had thumped to a landing near the base of the shaft. Owen was just lowering himself down, and the two children hugged each other with hardly any self-consciousness. Then they stepped back and exchanged a *W* handshake.

"Hey, everybody, keep up!" Baba Yaga shouted as the mortar stirred and was off again, pounding down the corridor. "It's still on the trail."

Hurriedly the dragon, warrior, Coyote, and two children (one with two pocketed tribbles) set off jogging down the corridor. Following the eagerly thumping mortar, they ignored cross corridors until they emerged into a great open plaza. Across it was what looked like the arched doorway to the hangar where they had first landed. But the sight between them and that doorway stopped them dead.

A vast assemblage of garbage cans stretched in a greenish brown mass. Glinting throughout were countless metallic weapons, some looking like the poles that had trapped them at first, some looking even more threatening. Mandy gazed about in despair. There was no way that enchantments, magic swords, or TV remotes could win out here.

Beside her, Owen sighed. "Dead end."

She shook her head. "Just plain dead."

After a long tense silence, one of the larger garbage cans stepped forward and began speaking in flabby English. "You have violated our hospitality and attempted to sabotage our ship. Damage reports are still coming in. Such irrational behavior is not tolerable. You are under arrest to await execution. Further resistance is useless."

From their little group, Coyote stepped forward, though as he was still partially wrapped in the cape, all that was visible was a floating head and tail.

"Hospitality! Ha! You violently confine a diplomatic delegation sent here to humanely warn you away from your doom. What you call sabotage is simply a casual expression of displeasure over our reception. But as you appear determined to pit your puny selves against our planet's diverse and infinitely greater power, we must simply give up on you and depart. Now step aside, if you please."

The garbage can hopped up and down. "Your planet is not superior! Our sensors have shown that your technology is primitive, and they have not shown people as odd and hard to control as you seem to be. You lie, and you will be conquered!"

Coyote laughed haughtily. "The ineffectiveness of your sensors just proves how weak you are. All they could detect is the rather basic technology still clung to by the simplest group of our planet's many inhabitants." He turned, jabbing a paw free from his invisibility and pointing at Mandy and

Owen. "You chose their language in which to communicate, probably because their feeble electronic broadcasts are the only ones you are capable of picking up.

"But in fact there are a great many species on our world with powers far greater than your own. 'Odd' doesn't begin to describe us, and our languages are as different as our technology."

Instantly he switched into a choppy musical language that Mandy figured must be some Indian tongue. Taking his lead, Baba Yaga launched into what sounded like a violent scolding in Russian. Norse and Chinese chimed in, and from Owen's pocket came an angry-sounding hum.

"Enough!" the lead can said. "Our computers can interpret any language, but what you say is not believable. It is not normal for one planet to have so many different creatures, or so many different languages. It is not normal to have different types of technology. Therefore, we do not believe you. Our universe is governed by laws of normality. What you say does not fit in. Therefore it is wrong."

Suddenly Mandy had had enough. They were doomed anyway, so what was there to lose? Angrily she stalked forward. "Wake up, garbage heads! You're the ones who've got things wrong. Normality is a big bore. The only thing that's basic to this universe seems to be weirdness. If you can't take that, then you'd better leave us alone!"

"Right on!" Owen exclaimed, and with a fierce karate yell he leaped to Mandy's side. For the heck of it, he did a few exhibition chops and lunges ending with a low spin and kick that thunked into the lead garbage can and sent it spinning back into the crowd like a hockey puck.

For seconds, everything remained frozen. Then sounds of blubbering outrage rolled through the crowd. Exchanging hopeless looks, the little party from Earth closed ranks.

Above them, Siegfried raised his gleaming sword. "There is no greater honor than a glorious death!"

"Depends on your options," Owen whispered.

"Haven't got any," Mandy replied.

Like a tidal wave, the alien mob surged forward. But suddenly their furious babbling was cut into by a new sound. From far down a corridor came a horn's haunting call. It was echoed by wild animal cries, like the baying of giant hounds. Then came howling wind, the dry clatter of metal on bone, and the growing thunder of galloping hooves.

At one end of the plaza a dark cloud flowed from a doorway: spectral riders, their tattered cloaks blowing in an icy wind, hell hounds baying at their feet. At their head, astride a great black horse, was the Wild Huntsman, the Lord of Fear, the Horned King. Antlers spread like claws from his helmeted head, and his deep sepulchral voice rolled forth in chanting song.

Mandy didn't know the words, she didn't want to know them. Their very sound pierced her with fear. They dripped with hopelessness, with visions of tombs and of dark empty lands where souls drifted on glacial winds, forever searching, forever lost.

At the apparition's sudden arrival, the crowd of angry aliens had fallen silent. Now there came an anguished moaning. Soft at first, it swelled into panic as garbage cans began shrinking away from that end of the room. The small clump of Earth folk was ignored, as the aliens surged for the exits.

The dark king with his terror-filled song continued his steady advance. Behind him, his riders spread out like mist. With death's head grins they gazed at the cowering creatures, their bony hands grasping out.

The surge became a stampede, and the terrified moaning was drowned out by the slapping of panicky feet.

125

Soon the great plaza was nearly empty. Only the huddled group from Earth remained. Slowly the Horned King rode toward them. Behind him, the skeletal hunters and their hounds thinned and vanished like mist.

He had ceased his anguished song. From out of his helmet, fiery eyes glowed down at them. His voice echoed hollowly.

"Let us go home."

CHAPTER FIFTEEN

WEIRD POWER

Baba Yaga was the first to recover. "Right," she said. "Home." With a determined thump of the pestle she began poling the mortar across the empty space toward the arched hangar entrance. The Horned King turned his horse after her and, still a little dazed, the others followed.

Inside the enormous hangar, the little Russian cottage looked very forlorn. But as soon as they entered the space, it jumped up on its chicken legs and scrambled toward them. Mandy and Owen looked at each other. It seemed to be clucking.

The little house hovered over Baba Yaga, who had climbed out of her mortar. The house actually quivered and probably would have hugged her if it could. Gruffly the old witch said, "Yes, yes, I'm happy to see you too. Now just sit down, deary, so we can climb in."

Owen, who'd been looking uneasily around, pointed to a large blank wall. "Hey, what about the exit. They've closed the side that opened into space."

"Time for an opening spell," Baba Yaga grunted. She

stomped toward the wall, the house trotting behind her like a puppy. The witch sang and chanted and hopped up and down, but nothing happened.

After a minute Siegfried said, "Step aside, venerable grandmother. This is a warrior's task." Raising his sword over his head, he gave the wall a mighty blow only to bounce off and land flat on his back. "Tough stuff," he muttered as Lung Nu helped him to his feet.

On impulse, Mandy fished the TV remote out of her pocket and randomly pressed buttons. With a grinding whine, one whole side of the giant room rose up and slid into the ceiling.

Mandy looked down at the gadget in her hands and tried to sound casual. "These things double as garage door openers, you know." She handed it back to Baba Yaga.

Minutes later, the brightly painted Russian cottage was fully occupied and scuttling through space as fast as its chicken legs could carry it. Once the alien ship had become a smudgy dot in the rear window, they all agreed it was more than time to eat something. Baba Yaga brought out or conjured up what she could, and for a while they alternated between stuffing themselves and exchanging excited accounts of their experiences.

At last, however, Coyote wiped his muzzle on a chair, stood up, and said, "I believe we all owe our Celtic colleague a vote of thanks for routing the enemy and letting us escape." The others nodded or grunted in agreement, and the Horned King, who was sitting again in his shadowed corner, actually seemed to smile.

"Apologies for the length of my absence. The paths to and from my Otherworld are faint at this distance. But it was not I who routed them. It was their own fear."

Lung Nu had returned to her human form and was sitting

on a bench beside Siegfried. Now she frowned thoughtfully. "But I do not fully understand that. Enlighten me. How can a people who are so unspiritual, so unimaginative, actually know fear? Does not fear require the imagining of what might happen in bad circumstances?"

The Horned King spoke quietly. "Indeed, I can tell you about fear. It is, after all, my special field. Truly, much fear does depend on imagination, and so those creatures would be immune to it. But fear of death—that is another matter."

Slowly he stood up, his great antlers barely clearing the rafters. "If one cannot imagine any life other than that which one knows, if one cannot envision any other possible plane of existence, then death is indeed a most fearful prospect. It seems final, absolute."

"But even humans, imaginative as they are, fear death," Lung Nu pointed out.

"True, but their fear rises from the uncertainty of the details. Every culture, every person holds a different view of death and of what may happen afterward. Yet they all possess enough imagination to accept that, whatever the details, some new plane of existence may await them. These pathetic aliens have no such comfort. They see nothing but emptiness, the ending of all things, and their fear rises from deepest despair."

"So how long will this fear you gave them last?" Mandy asked quietly.

The huntsman shrugged and slumped back into his dark corner. "Long enough to permit us to slip away, but not long enough to save our world,"

"Hey," Baba Yaga snapped. "What we don't need now is another dose of doom and gloom. I think we did pretty well by ourselves back there. We bollixed up their weather, nearly deafened them with appalling music, and gummed up their engines with zombie tribbles. By the way, Coyote, you haven't told us what you were up to all that time.''

The animal smiled roguishly. ''I found their navigation center. A cloak of invisibility is very useful when it comes to twisting dials and knobs that send folks off course.''

Shaking himself, Coyote stood up and began pacing around a little patch of floor. ''But it will really be only a temporary setback, all of it. We made a great team, but eventually they will get the lights turned on and the storms turned off. They'll straighten out their navigation, unplug the loud speakers, and vacuum up the fake tribbles. I wasn't lying totally in there. Our ''technology,'' magic, and imagination, may be superior to theirs, but only in a moral sense. They can still come in with that incredible war machine of theirs and beat the socks off humanity. I doubt that we've done much more than delay the end by a few days.''

After a time, Mandy got up and walked to the window. Owen joined her. Together they looked out at the glowing sphere of green and blue and swirling white coming ever closer. It hung like a precious gem against the blackness of space.

''Awfully pretty, isn't it?'' Mandy said softly.

''Do you think the invaders will find it as pretty as we do?'' Owen asked.

''Not a chance,'' Baba Yaga said, coming up behind them and placing bony hands on their shoulders. Neither flinched. ''They won't know a good thing when they see it. Besides, it's not just water and trees and rocks that make this place beautiful, it's all the people who've lived here and all the stuff they've dreamed about. Of course, you measly little mortals can't see it, but that world's surrounded by a lot more than clouds. All those Otherworlds are out there, wrapping the place in a glorious shimmering rainbow.

It's a crying shame those animated dumpsters are going to barge in and bust everything up!''

''But surely we will not allow them to do so without a fight,'' Lung Nu said standing up.

''No,'' Coyote agreed. ''We will all go back to the Otherworlds and rally support for a final battle. And Mandy and Owen's world will launch missiles and fighter planes at the invaders. Together maybe we'll hold out for hours or even days before they destroy most of us, and enslave the survivors.''

''Then we shall at least die nobly,'' Siegfried said as he stood towering over the Dragon Princess. ''Our last epic battle will be a glorious one.''

Coyote nodded. ''Probably, though there won't be many left to make legends about it.''

It was not a cheerful return trip, yet no one seemed anxious for it to end. Soon, however, the chicken house was skimming the boundaries of Earth's Otherworlds. Despite their unhappiness, Owen and Mandy stayed glued to the window and watched as their odd little craft scrambled down among cloud swirled crags and settled at the foot of an arched bridge. It stretched like a rainbow toward a towering castle, a construct of rock and clouds and frozen light.

Siegfried bade them all a dramatic farewell, then shared a few quiet words with Lung Nu as she stood with him in the doorway. Afterward, when they had departed, the Dragon Princess sat in shadowed silence until the cottage had come to rest on the shores of a wide silver lake.

As the princess bowed to them in formal farewell, Mandy wondered if it was really true that dragons could not cry. But perhaps that had only been the glitter of her black pearl earrings as Lung Nu dissolved herself into the form of a dragon. Sliding beneath the waters of the lake, she began swimming toward the palace of jade and pearl they could see gleaming far beneath the surface.

Coyote was let off in a land of dry rock and sage brush where the wind was hot. Flat-topped mesas rose in the distance, walls of gold and red etched against a sharp blue sky. In bewildering contrast, the Horned King slipped from the cottage door into a land of cold and gloom. Purple, cloud-shrouded mountains glowered over shadowed valleys and dark, wind-stirred forests. Moments after leaving them, his fearful antlered figure was swallowed up in damp swirling mists.

Then only the witch, the tribbles, and the two children remained. Looking at her last guests, Baba Yaga tried for a frightening cackle. "You two plump children aren't afraid to be alone with old Baba Yaga, now, are you?"

Boldly Owen grinned at her. "Don't give us that, you old softy." Then he reached into one pocket and pulled out a reddish brown tribble. "Here, if you promise not to eat it, I'd like you to have one of these."

Hesitantly she took the creature in one bony hand and after a moment began stroking it with the other. "All fur and no meat. It'll be good company while I watch TV."

None of them said what they were thinking: how there wouldn't be TV or anything else for much longer. When the house gave a little thump, Baba Yaga hurried to the door.

"All right you two, out! Look at the mess I've got to clean up. Can't stand houseguests. Can't stand farewells."

The two children jumped down the steps, then turned back just as the door was closing. "Bye, you old witch," Owen called, seeing an answering smile that was probably not as wicked as it was intended to be.

In a flurry, the house scrambled back onto its chicken

legs and scurried off through the trees. For a moment those trees looked like white birches; then they were only the old maples and oaks in the town's block-long park.

"Hermes, Iowa," Mandy said, looking around. "How long do you suppose we've been gone?"

"It felt like days, but you can never tell with magic—if you can believe the stories."

"You can believe them."

Owen nodded, looking beyond the trees to the buildings of downtown Hermes. "Looks pretty normal, doesn't it?"

"Yeah. I never knew 'normal' could look so good."

"We have been kind of pigging out on weirdness lately."

Mandy started to trudge off through the park. "Trouble is, it gets sort of hard to draw the line between weird and normal. Maybe there's really not a lot of point in trying. Maybe we should just take things as they come."

"There're some things that are coming, I'd just as soon not take."

Uneasily Mandy looked up at the clear autumn sky. "How long do you think we have?"

"A couple of days, a couple of hours. I don't know."

"Do you think they'll blow the emergency sirens like for tornadoes?"

"Maybe. Maybe the president will come on TV and tell everyone we're about to be blown out of the universe but to please stay calm."

"Maybe he's on TV right now."

Their pace had already moved from a walk to a trot. Now it became a run. Out of breath, they reached Olympia Towers Apartments, and Owen fumbled in the bin below the mailboxes. "Here's Mr. Bender's newspaper. He never picks it up till evening. Yep, it's still Saturday. The same date all right. Jeez, I guess it really was some sort of magic time warp.''

Through the doors on one of the downstairs apartments, they could hear a serious TV news voice. Looking at each other, they charged for the stairs, Owen peeling off at the fifth floor while Mandy sped on to the seventh.

Charging down the hall she was hit by a great need to be surrounded by her normal family in her normal apartment. And more than anything, she wanted there not to be space invaders coming to take it all away, normal and weird alike.

After bursting open the apartment door, Mandy stood still a moment, taking it all in. Her mother setting the table for supper, her dad watching the TV news, her baby brother sitting in a corner of his playpen holding a one-sided conversation with his pink bunny.

She didn't want to look at it, but the TV drew her like a magnet. Walking over to the couch she plopped down beside her dad and hugged him. Then flatly she asked, ''What's going on?''

''On the news? Oh, really big stuff. Everyone is pretty shaken up.''

''Yeah, I bet they are.''

''They've been interviewing a bunch of experts, though, and they think they can stop it.''

''They think they can stop this! How?''

''Well, watch the TV. Don't quiz me about it.''

Reluctantly, she did. A perfectly groomed woman was talking to a bald man with a beard wearing a suit that looked rather too large for him. He was rubbing his nose nervously.

''Well, Margaret, whoever this computer hacker is, he's awfully good. He, or she, of course, knows every nation's computer system well enough to get his message onto every screen on this planet. And he's clearly not your average teenage computer whiz. I mean, look at the languages he's chosen to broadcast in. Not only English this time, but also Old Norse, Classical Chinese, Russian, Navaho, and something that appears to be ancient Welsh. I mean, that's a mind-boggling spread.''

"No more mind-boggling than the message, professor."

"True enough. Some people think it's supposed to be tied to that last hoax message about space invaders. My own theory is that it's a coded message for some crime syndicate or something. I mean, what could anyone possibly intend by something like that?''

He turned and pointed to a screen where the studio engineers had just flashed up the message received on computers all over the world. "People of Earth. Have reevaluated. Invasion is canceled. You are too weird."

Mandy sat up and stared at the TV. "That's it? They sent that message in Russian and Old Welsh and all those other languages?''

Her father yawned. "Yeah. Is that weird or what?''

As Mandy sat in stunned silence, her father continued. "And the news item before this one was just as weird. Scientists are tearing their hair because that comet they were so hot to study has just changed course, which they insist comets are not supposed to do, and . . .''

Mandy didn't listen any further. She leaped up and ran out onto the balcony. The sun had set, leaving the clear autumn sky a darkening shade of violet. Silhouetted against it was a single slender column with its bronze statue of the god Hermes forever poised in midstride. Above, the first stars were coming out, glints of light shining brighter by the moment.

A sharp whistle rose from below. Mandy looked over

the railing and saw Owen grinning up at her from a balcony two stories down. He raised his hand in a *W*. Grinning back, Mandy did the same.

"Hey," he called, "since there *is* going to be a tomorrow, let's get to work on those papers."

"Right on! We sure have done some majorly weird research."

Just then, Owen's mother called that their tofu stew was ready. He grimaced, flashed a final salute, and disappeared inside.

Feeling vastly happy, Mandy looked up again. The Hermes column had almost faded into darkness, while overhead the stars were brightening and beginning to spangle across the sky.

Gazing into them, she was just as glad not to see any fleeing comets, but she did recognize one of the usual constellations. Just plain stars, no mythical picture. Yet suddenly its message was clear. It was Cassiopeia, the one that the star books describe as looking like a big *M*. Now, however, she knew that the books had it upside down.

"It was a *W*. A big celestial *W*—up there forever, watching over this world. Watching over its people and any other worlds they cared to dream up.